YOU'RE THE
Reason
J. NATHAN

This book is a work of fiction. Names, characters, places, and incidents are the product of the author's imagination or are used fictitiously and are not considered to be real. Any resemblance to actual events, locales, or persons, living or dead, is coincidental.

Copyright © 2020 by J. Nathan

Edited by Stephanie Elliot
Proofed by Gem's Precise Proofreads

Cover Design by Kate Farlow at Y'all. That Graphic.
Cover Photo by Michelle Lancaster @lanefotograf
Cover Model Andy Murray

First Edition June 2020

*For my wonderful assistant, Renee McCleary.
Thank you for all you do to keep me sane, make me laugh,
and encourage me to write the kind of stories my readers
love. I am so lucky to have you in my life.*

CHAPTER ONE

"It was less than a year ago that sorority pledge Sydney Lane plunged four stories to her death just feet from where I stand outside Harris Hall…"

I flinched at the reporter's words as I pulled another box from the back of my mom's SUV, trying to stay out of the cameraman's shot. Having my face flashed across the news, while a reporter rehashed the gruesome details of Sydney Lane's death, was not my idea of a great first day at a new school.

"Sydney's family continues to believe their daughter would never take her own life," the reporter continued, "but the university stands by their investigation with local authorities claiming there was no evidence of foul play."

Only those living under a rock hadn't heard the story of Sydney Lane, the homecoming queen from Austin, Texas, who died while pledging the Alpha Phi sorority her freshman year.

"Reporting to you live from Crestwood University," the reporter said before throwing it back to the news station.

My mother slammed the back of her SUV and lifted one of the boxes. "Let's go meet your roommate."

I slung my backpack over my shoulders then lifted two boxes, balancing the lighter one on top of the heavier one.

"You sure you got those?" my mom asked.

"Mom, I'm fine. That was over a year ago."

She sighed.

I knew she worried about me, but I really was fine.

I followed her toward the propped-open front door of Harris Hall, an old brick dorm in need of some updating. I hadn't toured Crestwood's campus before transferring because being closer to home was all that mattered. Put me in a room in Texas, and I'd make it work. I hadn't even spoken with my new roommate, having reached out but never receiving a reply. I assumed it was an old email address and shrugged it off knowing I'd make that work too.

My knee felt only a little stiff as we climbed three flights of stairs to the third floor and followed the numbers to 320. The door was open and the room had already been decorated, except for the bed with the bare mattress by the left wall and empty desk that I assumed was for me.

I set the boxes on the floor and scanned the small space. My roommate had hung tiny strands of white lights around the room. Her paisley comforter was adorned with small matching throw pillows and a teddy bear with an Alpha Phi shirt on it. The board on the wall above her desk was filled with photos. I moved closer to get a better look. The blonde in every photo with the perfect cheekbones and impeccable curls had to be my roommate. Her friends all looked similar to her, and many wore Alpha Phi shirts.

"Hey, y'all," a sweet voice greeted us.

I spun on my red Converse and found the living version of the girl in the photos standing in the doorway looking just as beautiful in person. "Hi."

She had green eyes and a warm smile. "You must be my new roommate," she said, nodding in the direction of the boxes I had placed on the floor.

I smiled, my blue eyes nowhere near as vibrant as her green and my brown hair nowhere near as perfectly curled as hers. "I'm Sophia."

"I'm Chantel."

"I'm Mom," my mom added.

Chantel chuckled. "Nice to meet you, Mrs. Galloway."

My eyes narrowed. Neither my mom nor I had said our last name. *Had* she gotten my email and just not replied?

Noticing my confusion, Chantel added, "Our RA just told me your name. That *is* your last name, isn't it?" Her eyes jumped curiously between my mom and me.

"Yeah. I just transferred from the University of Maine."

She dropped down onto her bed. "Didn't like the snow?"

I laughed. "Hated it."

"Are you a sophomore, too?" my mother asked her.

"I'm a senior." Something clouded her sparkly eyes, and a distant look filled them. "It's a long story."

Knowing when not to pry, my mom and I made small talk with her about our intended majors—history for me and communications for her—then excused ourselves a short time later to retrieve the remainder of my belongings from the car. When we returned, Chantel wasn't there.

After helping me make my bed and unpack my clothes, my mom said goodbye. There was something so comforting about knowing she'd only be forty-five minutes away.

I heaved a sigh as recollections of my time in Maine flashed through my mind. The lonely nights. The meals alone. The long FaceTime calls with anyone back home who'd answer. I was a country girl suddenly transplanted to a snow-covered state where everyone skied and loved the cold weather except me. Being that far from home had taken an emotional toll on me, so I decided to transfer closer to home. Hence starting a new school in Houston for my sophomore year.

I unpacked my own small collage of photos in a frame and hung it above my desk. Though I had a handful of close friends back home, I still hoped to make new friends here in Houston. I wasn't a social butterfly, like I gathered my roommate was, but I also wasn't a recluse.

"Thank God, we're finally alone," Chantel said, sweeping back into the room and closing the door behind her. "Tell me everything." She dropped down onto her bed. "You single, bi, doing the long-distance thing, playing the field? Go."

My eyes went wide, taken aback by the once sweet girl my mom had met. This version was nosy as hell. "Um…"

"You planning on pledging a sorority?"

"Um…"

"I've got pull with the Alpha Phis. It's the best sorority on campus."

"Is that your sorority?"

She laughed like I should've known that. "Obviously."

"You don't have a house?"

Something darkened in her expression, just like it had before when my mom was still there. "Not this year."

I said nothing, realizing I must've put my foot in my mouth.

"Sydney Lane was pledging our sorority," she explained. "And since her family won't accept Sydney's death was a suicide and won't give up their investigation, the university shut down our house for the year to appease them." Her eyes drifted over the four walls of our room. "That's why I'm back in this hell hole. No offense."

I shrugged. It didn't matter to me. I was back in Texas. That's all I cared about. "Are your sorority sisters in this dorm, too?"

"Yeah" she clipped. "All of us punished because of Sydney's decision."

"You didn't want to live with any of *them*?" I asked, treading lightly.

"My bestie Patrice transferred last minute. That's why you lucked out and got this room with me—Enough talk. You up for a party tonight?" she asked.

"Oh, I…"

"It's settled." She stood. "You're coming."

"Where's the party?"

She cocked her head. "Does it matter?"

I chuckled. "I guess not."

"I'm gonna go hang with my girls while you finish unpacking. I'll come back to get ready and get you. We'll have drinks in their room, then head over to Kappa Sigma."

"Sounds good," I said, not really sure I was up for a party with a group of girls I didn't know, but I was willing to give it a try.

Once she disappeared out the door, I could finally breathe. Between her looks and rapid-fire questioning, she commanded an audience and dominated a conversation. I wasn't used to someone so…forward. But she was my new roommate, so I'd make it work.

* * *

I curled my normally straight hair and threw on skinny jeans and an off-the-shoulder navy shirt, hoping to make my blue eyes pop. I brushed on a little blush and swiped on some mascara, making my already long lashes extend further. I was in the midst of curling my eyelashes when Chantel breezed into the room a little before nine.

"Almost ready?" she asked as she pulled off her T-shirt in front of the closet, sans bra.

"Yup." I averted my eyes as she took her time searching for a shirt. If only I had that much confidence.

"I can't wait to introduce you to my sorority sisters."

I focused on curling my eyelashes, not wanting to turn around until I was sure she was dressed.

"How do I look?" she asked.

I held my breath as I twisted around. *Phew*. She stood there in a short denim skirt and a white crop top that showed not only her toned stomach but accentuated her perfect boobs. "Nice."

"Is that what you're wearing?" she asked, a tinge of disapproval in her tone as her eyes drifted over my outfit.

I glanced down. "Do I not look all right?"

She hesitated. "You look fine."

Her words played through my mind again as we entered her sorority sisters' room on the fourth floor. The space was the same size as ours but filled with girls all wearing the same outfit—tiny denim skirts but different colored crop tops. Apparently, I hadn't gotten the memo.

All conversations ceased and eyes turned toward me. The girls assessed me from head to toe. I'd never felt more uncomfortable in my life, knowing a roomful of sorority girls were sizing me up all at once.

"Hi," they said in unison, breaking into a bout of laughter once they realized how they sounded.

I lifted my hand. "Hey."

Chantel closed the door behind us and bottles of wine were passed around. A few girls asked about my sophomore status and where I lived, but besides that, I sat back and listened to them chat about guys, their summers, who they planned to hook up with this year, and rush week coming up soon. It was obvious Chantel was their leader. She ruled the conversation, and they all quieted when she spoke.

"So, Maine, huh?" the only other brunette in the room asked as she sat down beside me on the floor.

"Yup."

"Didn't like the cold?" she asked.

I shook my head, realizing I'd have to have the same conversation with each new person I met. "Not at all."

She laughed. "I'm Valerie."

"Sophia."

"Yeah, I know. Chantel filled us in before you got here."

I cringed.

"Don't worry," she smiled. "It wasn't bad."

"I heard she was supposed to have another roommate. I hope she's not too upset she got stuck with me instead."

I expected Valerie to laugh and tell me Chantel was excited to have me, but she didn't. She shrugged.

My eyes widened. "She *is* pissed."

Valerie grinned. "She would've *loved* a single."

Freaking great.

A short time later we walked across campus, the loud cackles from the large group carrying through the darkness. I felt like an outsider as I followed behind, trying to politely listen to their conversations but saying very little.

We moved toward a large white house with black shutters. A big Greek K hung on the peaked roof above the second floor. The rumble of loud music playing inside the house vibrated the pavement beneath our feet as we moved up the sidewalk.

"Hey!" called a guy from the front door.

The girls waved or called back to him.

He turned his head and shouted inside, "The Alpha Phis are here. Lock the door to the roof."

Knots of unease formed in my stomach. Had he actually just made a joke about Sydney Lane's death? I glanced around and none of the girls seemed angry about his comment. My eyes collided with Valerie's. Her twisted lips told me she was the only one who understood my surprise—and disgust.

We reached the front door, held open by the jerk who'd made the comment. The girls all filed inside, greeting him as they passed by. I moved through the doorway last, purposely stepping on his foot on my way by. "Oops."

His death glare told me he knew I'd done it on purpose. *Huh.* He was smarter than I gave him credit for.

Chantel led the way as I trailed the girls, wondering why I agreed to go to a party in the first place. This really wasn't my thing. We walked down a crowded hallway where guys and girls drank from red cups, turning their bodies to make room for us to move by. Guys ogled the Alpha Phis, while the other girls—who probably just realized they'd have competition—looked away in disgust.

We passed through an open door at the end of the hallway that led down a small set of stairs. Music reverberated through the tight stairwell which eventually opened up to a large basement. Guys and girls danced in the middle of the tiled floor while others drank and mingled around the room or at the bar that lined the back wall.

Many heads turned when the Alpha Phis paraded in. The girls definitely loved the attention, but I wondered if they loved each other. They were friendly, but I couldn't tell if they were friends or just acting the part.

I veered from the group and took a spot by the wall, checking my phone.

"You need a drink?"

I glanced up to find a guy with a shaved head holding out a cup.

I eyed the cup. "No offense, but I've seen too many Lifetime movies to know there could be something other than flat beer in that cup."

He laughed, downing the contents of the cup to show he hadn't laced the beer.

"One can never be too safe. Predators come in all shapes and sizes," I assured him.

He laughed again. "Let's get you a cup straight from the keg."

I nodded.

He walked me to the bar, calling to a guy to pour me a beer.

I watched the guy pour it before he handed it to me. "Thanks," I said before turning to Mr. Shaved Head. "I'm Soph—" But he'd disappeared.

O-kay.

I moved back to the side of the room and drank my beer as I watched Chantel and her sisters dance on the dance floor, some with guys and some in a group together.

Chantel had her arms wrapped tightly around a tall guy who had his face buried in her neck. I couldn't see his face, but my guess was he was either the president of the frat or the best-looking guy in that dark basement. Chantel didn't seem the type to settle for anything less. His massive arms were wrapped around her waist, and he must've been doing or saying something to elicit the laughter tumbling out of her.

I spotted some of the other girls dancing together. Valerie, though just as pretty as the others, looked out of place in the group. Maybe it was her dark hair. Or, maybe it was the strange way her eyes looked devoid of light around the other girls. One on one, she seemed fine. But in the middle of the group, she looked…uncomfortable.

"Drink up," the guy with the shaved head said, leaning against the wall beside me again. "It's a party. Have fun."

He was right. I did need some fun in my life. I tipped back my cup and downed my beer.

"And just like that, she's here to party," my new friend announced as I wiped the foam off my top lip with the back of my hand. "I'm Ryan."

"Sophia," I said as a wave of warmth spread through my body thanks to the beer coursing through it. "I just transferred."

He nodded like he understood. "Well, let's go get you another beer."

A few beers later, I found myself in the middle of the dance floor dancing with Valerie and some of the other girls. I was laughing and actually having fun, and I knew, besides being totally buzzed, I was happier here than I'd ever been in Maine.

A hand grasped hold of my wrist, catching me off guard. I twisted around to find Ryan tugging on my arm and leading me off the dance floor. "What are you doing?"

"Let's go play pool."

I laughed to myself as I let him lead me upstairs to the main floor where a group of guys and girls stood around a pool table, using it as a seat or a place to set down their drinks.

"All right people, move it!" he called.

They hopped off the table, clearing the way for us to play. "I need to show Maine how we do things in Texas."

My head whipped back. "Maine?"

"Word travels fast at a school this size."

"I'm actually from Texas," I assured him, a little unsettled that people I didn't know already knew about me.

He racked up the balls on the table. "Ladies first—unless you need me to show you how it's done."

I slipped a pool stick off the rack on the wall. "I think I can manage." I lined up my shot on the table then glanced to Ryan who seemed to be staring at my ass. "Do I do it like this?" I asked, feigning oblivion.

His eyes jumped from my ass to my eyes. "Uh huh."

I tapped my pool stick into the cue ball. The triangle of colorful balls split apart, landing in all directions on the table. Two of the striped balls buried themselves in the corner pockets at the far side of the table.

"Nice break," Ryan said, his eyes scanning the pool table. "Looks like you're stripes."

"Are those the ones with the stripes on them?" I asked facetiously.

He threw back his head and laughed. "You're a ringer, aren't you?"

I smiled, then proceeded to sink every one of the striped balls. I'd grown up with a pool table in my basement. So, I knew my way around a table, but Ryan took it like a champ, slapping my hand and getting me another drink after my victory.

Somewhere around midnight, I found myself puking alone in the front yard. Thankfully, no one else had ventured out to witness the grace that was my drunken self.

I stumbled my way over to the curb and sat down. My head throbbed and my stomach roiled, though I couldn't imagine anything was left inside me. I pulled a pack of wintergreen gum from my pocket and stuffed three pieces into my mouth, contemplating my next move.

I could go back in and let Chantel know I was leaving, if she even noticed I disappeared. I could *try* to walk back to the dorm without face-planting somewhere along the way—if I could *remember* the way back. Or, I could call an Uber in hopes that they knew where my dorm was.

"What the fuck are you doing?" a deep voice called, cutting through the silent darkness.

My body stiffened.

Footsteps approached, and a tall guy with dark hair and light blue eyes stood there, glaring down at me. "I said what are you doing?"

"No, you said what the *fuck* are you doing."

His eyes absorbed the details of my face with disdain. "You didn't answer my question."

"What's your problem? You scared your little party's gonna get broken up if someone sees me out here?" I gasped mockingly. "All that wasted beer and unused condoms. The horror."

His eyes narrowed. "Is that supposed to be funny?"

"Not any funnier than *you* out here reprimanding me, frat boy."

He dragged his hands through his hair as his head dropped back. "What the fuck?"

I unsteadily pushed myself to my feet, praying to God I didn't fall face first in front of him. "No worries, frat boy. I was leaving anyway."

He grabbed my arm, his grip tight as he stopped me from going anywhere. "Don't come back here."

A wave of nausea washed over me. "Excuse me?"

He clenched his teeth. "You're not an Alpha Phi which makes you unwelcome here."

A cold chill rushed up my spine, but I maintained my composure. "No problem. Your party sucked anyway." I turned and walked in the direction I hoped my dorm was in, putting one foot in front of the other and trying to appear steady. Because despite his harsh tone and rudeness, the bastard stood on the curb, watching me until I disappeared into the darkness.

CHAPTER TWO

"Where'd you take off to?" Chantel asked as she breezed through the door of our room the following morning. She wore the same clothes she'd worn the previous night, but looked no less put together.

I sat up, trying not to puke as the sunlight filtering into the room intensified my throbbing headache. "Y'all were having so much fun. I didn't want to bother you."

"Did you hook up with anyone?" Chantel asked, slipping out of her wedges.

"Um, no."

"Not even Ryan?" She shimmied out of her denim skirt and stood there in a tiny thong—as if it were normal to walk around someone you just met that way. "I saw you talking to him."

"He was nice. Just not really my type."

She grabbed her bathrobe and slipped into it. "What *is* your type?"

I shrugged. "I guess I'll know when I meet him."

She turned to the closet and retrieved her toiletries.

"How long have you been with your boyfriend?" I asked.

"I don't have a boyfriend," she said.

"Oh, I just thought the guy you danced with…and then you didn't come home…"

She laughed as she turned to me. "I *want* Chase to be my boyfriend. But he's so busy with frat stuff and family stuff. He said if he had time for a girlfriend, it would be me."

I nodded, understanding not wanting to string someone along if you had a full plate.

"Doesn't mean I won't make him change his mind," she said with a sly smile.

I laughed, knowing from the brief time we'd spent together, that Chantel was someone who definitely got what she wanted.

* * *

Chantel slept soundly as I slipped out of our dorm room on Monday morning. Being a transfer student, I got whatever classes were available—which meant eight o'clock classes every morning for me.

I trekked across campus, admiring the beauty of the quad—the old cobblestone buildings with their castle-topped roofs and sidewalks lined with blooming magnolia trees. I pulled in a breath of fresh air, albeit ninety-five-degree air, but it wasn't accompanied by a puff of cold air leaving my mouth like most mornings in Maine.

I found Roper Hall and climbed the steps to the old building, scanning the room numbers as I hurried down the nearly empty hallway. I stepped inside the classroom, realizing I must've been the only one who wanted to be early on their first day because all thirty desks sat empty.

Not wanting to be an overachiever, I moved toward the back of the room and slipped into the last seat in the second row.

Other students entered the room a short time later, taking seats all around the classroom until every desk was filled.

An older professor walked in and dropped his briefcase loudly on the front desk, purposely grabbing all of our attention. He handed out papers to the first person in each row, which they passed back to us, then addressed the class. "I'm Professor Irons. This is History 356, aka History through Film. If you're in the wrong place, this is your one chance to escape."

The girl in the desk beside mine grabbed her bag and hurried out of the room, nearly knocking over the guy stepping through the door at the same time.

"Whoa," he laughed as she hurried off. "The class that bad?" he called after her.

Everyone around me snickered as he stepped into the classroom, his cool swagger and easy smile an attention grabber. He eyed the room for an available seat, spotting the only one beside me. His blue eyes cut to mine, narrowing upon contact.

Frat boy.

Visible annoyance swept over his features, and I couldn't for the life of me figure out what I did to him to elicit such disdain. He walked down the first aisle and slouched into the last seat next to me, his long legs extending into the aisle.

I tried to focus on the professor and his lecture on the depiction of historical battles in films, but the pull to look beside me clawed at my sanity. What had I done to this guy? I hadn't even seen him inside the party. Had he really been that concerned that I might risk getting their party broken up?

As much as I hated to admit it, the darkness outside the frat house hadn't done the asshole justice. He was hot as hell. All built and stylish without even trying. And those lips, so perfect and full. Now I understood what people meant when they used a cupid's bow to describe someone's lips. Such a waste of hotness on someone so evil.

Professor Irons played a clip of a war in an old black and white movie I'd never heard of, pointing out the accuracy of the soldiers' formation as they stormed an enemy field.

Unable to stop myself, I looked to frat boy and whispered, "What's your problem?"

He turned to look at me with that same angry scowl I saw the night of the party. "What?"

"I'm not whoever you think I am."

He rolled his eyes.

Asshole. "Well, there's gotta be a reason you're such a jerk."

He scoffed before his blue eyes focused back on the movie, just in time to see the soldier on screen get impaled with a bayonet.

Oh, the irony.

"Perfection," Professor Irons said as he turned off the clip, flipped on the light, and dismissed us with the promise of an upcoming project.

I slipped my laptop into my bag and stood up. Frat boy had already left. *Good riddance.*

The remainder of my day was a lot less eventful, as frat boy wasn't in any of my other classes. I stopped by a campus coffee shop, grabbed a coffee and bagel, and sat at a table in the back. In no rush to get back to the dorm, I pulled out my laptop and typed the first paragraph of my essay for my Women and Literature course.

"Hey," Chantel said, appearing out of nowhere. "How was your first day?"

"Oh, hey. Good."

She smiled, not a hair out of place on her head as usual, whereas I'd been up since seven-thirty and had a nest for a ponytail.

"How were your classes?" I asked her.

"My first class starts at two."

"Note to self. No eight o'clock classes for me next semester."

She smiled. "Well, I just wanted to say hey when I spotted you back here. And to make sure you weren't avoiding me."

"No," I assured her. "I just find I work better with a little noise."

She winked. "I was just kidding. Maybe we can grab dinner tonight."

"Sure. That sounds great."

* * *

A few hours later, I entered the code on our door and it unlocked. I pushed it open and stumbled back a couple of steps when I found frat boy sprawled out on my bed. "What the hell are you doing in here?"

"Ummm," Chantel said.

My eyes shot to her standing in front of the mirror on our closet door.

"He's with me."

My face fell, a hundred thoughts playing through my mind.

"This is Chase," Chantel said. "Didn't I introduce you at the party?"

I removed my backpack and placed it on my desk chair. "Nope." I glanced to him, unmoving on my bed. "Do you mind?"

"*Chase*, that's Sophia's bed," Chantel said, urging him to move with her tone of voice.

He didn't. "You don't mind me laying here, do you Sophia?" he asked, his voice all deep and smooth, knowing full well I wanted his ass off my bed and out of my room.

"Actually, I do. I've always been taught frat boys carry STDs."

Chantel laughed. Chase didn't.

"Sophia's a history major just like you," Chantel informed him.

He didn't respond, just stared at me with those blue eyes, all cold and narrowed.

"I'm ready," she said, turning and walking toward the door. "Let's go."

He swung his legs off my bed and stood, his towering figure imposing in our small space. He was nauseatingly good looking. His T-shirt stretched across his sculpted chest, and the sleeves molded around his muscular biceps. He was definitely an athlete.

Chantel pulled open the door. "See you later, Sophia."

"Don't catch anything," I called as Chase followed her into the hallway without giving me another look.

The door clicked shut behind them. I stared at the door for a long time, my mind reeling.

Frat Boy was Chantel's man.

I needed that thought to settle for a bit. But it didn't make any sense. Why did the sight of me elicit such a cold reaction in him? Did Chantel not like me? Had I ruined her plan to have a single room this year? Had he planned to stay over every night and now he couldn't?

What the hell?

This was definitely not the start to the year I'd been hoping for.

CHAPTER THREE

I found myself wandering Baker Hall the following day searching for room 500. It didn't help that the room numbers didn't go in any certain order, jumping from 520 to 505.

"Sophia?"

I spun around to find Valerie walking toward me. Her hair was pulled back in a tight ponytail really showing her dark eyes and heart-shaped face. "Hey."

"You look lost."

"It's that obvious?"

She laughed. "Where are you headed?"

I held up the schedule on my phone. "Room 500."

"That's a lecture hall. It's down there at the end."

I sighed. "Thanks. You don't happen to be in Art History, do you?"

She shook her head. "Already took it. Let me know if you have Professor Barnes, and I'll share my notes from last year."

"Thanks."

A large group passed by, heading to the lecture hall.

"I better go get a seat."

"Okay," she said. "Do you wanna grab dinner tonight? I can stop by on my way to the dining hall."

"Sure."

"Great. See ya later." With that, she spun away and hurried down the hallway.

I headed in the opposite direction, finding the lecture hall at the end of the hall. I stepped through the door, and the room opened up to a five-hundred seat auditorium. I started up the stairs toward the back of the room, preferring to always sit in the back row. Unfortunately, every seat was taken. So, I relented, slipping into the aisle seat of the second to last row.

As more students made their way into the lecture hall, I scrolled through the newsfeed on my phone, checking on the college soccer scores at my friends' schools.

"Okay, settle in everyone. I'm Professor Barnes and this is Art History."

I tucked my phone away and looked to the female professor. Something out of the corner of my eye caught my attention.

Freaking great.

Chase.

He was staring at me from the opposite side of the room.

I refrained from flipping him the bird and averted my gaze.

This campus clearly wasn't big enough for the two of us.

* * *

I was watching Netflix on our television when someone knocked on the door. I rolled off my bed and hurried to answer it.

Valerie stood there. "Ready for dinner?

"Oh, right."

Her face fell. "Did you forget?"

I shook my head. Since Chantel blew me off the night before for Chase, and I ended up eating alone, I figured that Valerie only offered to be nice and wouldn't show. "Let me just throw on my shoes."

The walk to the dining hall was a quick one, but enough time for Valerie to fill me in on her first couple of days of classes. Inside, we both grabbed a sandwich. I nabbed a piece of chocolate cake before we made our way over to a small table by the window overlooking the campus.

"This is a lot nicer than my last school's dining hall," I said, glancing around the vast space. Hungry students sat at long tables and music played softly from speakers. "It's bigger and there are so many more food options."

"If you're a Texas girl, what made you go to Maine?" Valerie asked before biting into her sandwich.

I contemplated letting her in. Letting her know what a huge mistake I made by leaving Texas. Letting her in on what I'd lost because of it. But in the end, I just kept it simple. "I thought I needed to get away."

"Now?"

"I'm definitely a Texas girl." I pressed my fork into my cake and took a bite, savoring the sweet taste of chocolate coating my tongue.

"Dessert before dinner?" she asked.

"Chocolate trumps everything else."

She smiled. "Are you liking it here at Crestwood?"

"So far."

"And how about Chantel?" she asked with her mouth full. "How are you two getting along?"

"Honestly, I barely see her. Our schedules are completely opposite, and then she has Chase."

Valerie rolled her eyes.

"Uh, oh. What's that mean?"

She shook her head, her eyes growing distant. "I don't know why she hasn't moved on yet. He doesn't want her."

"He was over yesterday," I countered.

She shrugged. "He gets lonely. He dials her up."

"What's his story? Is he a senior too?"

"Yeah." She took another bite of her sandwich and spoke with a mouthful again. "He transferred second semester last year from Washington and was already a brother at their chapter of Kappa Sigma. Though, I always get the impression he doesn't really enjoy being in the frat. But then again, look at me. Sorority sister for life."

"Why *did* you join? You seem…different from the others."

"My mom was a sister." Disappointment swept across her features. "So, I'm a legacy. It was expected."

I ate more of my cake.

"Are you planning to rush?"

I shook my head. "Sororities aren't really my thing— no offense."

She laughed. "None taken."

"And, I can't really see myself agreeing to do all those ridiculous pledge things you've gotta do just to get in."

A mixture of regret and shame flashed across her eyes.

Shit. Why was I always saying the wrong thing? "So, I've told you about me. Tell me about you."

Valerie's face lit up. "Me?"

I laughed. "Yeah. Where are you from? What do you like to do?"

She spoke for the next fifteen minutes, barely coming up for air. It was as if no one had ever asked her about herself. And that light I thought was missing from her eyes the other night, shined brightly for the remainder of our dinner. We laughed—almost cried—as she told stories about all the beauty pageants her mom entered her in growing up and how she tried sabotaging every last one because she hated them so much. Valerie seemed like someone who'd been forced into situations she didn't want to be in. But the longer we spoke, the more I saw she was working on shedding that habit. And with me by her side, I had a feeling I'd get to know, and grow to really love, the real Valerie.

CHAPTER FOUR

I arrived early to History through Film the next morning, taking my seat in the back of the small classroom. Students filled the room over the next five minutes. Chase wasn't one of them.

I slipped my laptop out as Professor Irons set up a movie clip. He asked us to look for the various instances where art imitated life.

I pulled up a blank doc on my computer and began recording my findings as the clip played.

The classroom door creaked open a few minutes into the clip. My focus remained on my computer screen as Chase slipped into the seat beside me. I did my best to ignore him, my eyes jumping between the movie clip and my computer screen.

"What are we doing?" Chase whispered to me.

I glanced over with a raised brow, then turned back to the movie.

"You're not gonna tell me?"

I typed the words the actor uttered on my computer.

Chase leaned over to see my computer screen. "What does that mean?"

I turned my computer away from his prying eyes.

The girl in the seat in front of him twisted around and gladly offered up the assignment.

His looks are a disguise, sweetheart. The guy's a total jerk.

Once class ended, I closed my computer and stood up.

"Thanks for nothing," Chase muttered from his seat.

I gave him a sidelong glance. "Seriously?"

"Someone needs help and your reaction is to ignore them?" he asked.

If he thought he could make me feel bad for my behavior, he had another thing coming. "If memory serves me right, it sounds *exactly* like what happened outside your frat when you told me to leave."

He scoffed as he pushed himself to his feet, towering over me by a foot. His blue eyes riveted between mine. "It's gonna be a long fucking semester." He walked away, leaving anger clawing at my insides and my pulse thrashing against my skin.

* * *

"Put those by the far side of the tent," Chantel called to Valerie and me.

We rolled our eyes at each other as we carried boxes from Chantel's Mercedes to the huge white function tent in the sorority house's backyard. Chantel had guilt-tripped me into helping her since half her sisters were in class until five, and her rush event started at seven.

"Is she sure this is okay?" I asked Valerie as we passed by the yellow caution tape wrapped around the front lawn.

Valerie shrugged. "She claims no one said we couldn't be *outside* our house."

"Does it make you uncomfortable being here?" I asked, knowing Sydney Lane's death was the reason the house was closed for the year.

"A little." She stepped ahead of me, walking faster. I took that to mean she didn't want to discuss Sydney.

We walked under the tent weaving around the ten round tables covered with white linen tablecloths. Vases of fresh flowers sat in the center of each table. If I didn't know this was for a sorority rush event, I would've thought it was for a wedding. We put the boxes down on the ground in the corner of the tent.

"Careful with those!" Chantel shouted.

We spun around, thinking we'd done something wrong, but Chantel was yelling at some frat guys who were helping set up the white wooden folding chairs around each table.

I whispered to Valerie. "Is she always this bossy?"

Valerie nodded. "House or no house. She's not about to let anything ruin her reign as sorority president."

"Tina!" Chantel shouted to Valerie's roommate, currently fixing the flowers on the tables. "If any of those vases spill, it's on you."

Once Chantel turned back around, Tina mimicked her.

"I'm serious," Chantel said, her stern tone meaning she meant business. "These girls might not be getting the whole Alpha Phi experience this year, but the Alpha Phis *will* remain the best sorority this college has ever seen." Once her Elle Wood's worthy speech ended, Chantel pulled a long strand of lights out of one of the boxes. "Valerie! Hang these all around the tent."

Valerie inhaled a long breath in an effort to stay calm then walked over to Chantel, yanking the lights from her hand.

"Watch it, Val," Chantel said through gritted teeth.

My eyes narrowed as I watched their interaction.

Sensing me watching, Chantel's eyes flicked to me. Once she noticed she had an audience, she smiled at

Valerie and her tone changed. "You wouldn't want to break any of the bulbs."

Valerie said nothing to Chantel as she turned and walked away. "Are you sure you don't want to rush the Alpha Phis, Sophia?" Valerie said as she passed by me with the lights.

It wasn't a real question. She knew I'd be just fine without "sisters." Especially, bossy sisters who thought they ruled the world.

* * *

Chase burst into Friday's class late again. This time he leaned forward and asked the girl in front of him what our assignment was for the film clip that was playing. She showed him the directions. Not once did he look my way, which was fine by me. So was the fact that I hadn't found him on my bed or in my room lately.

At the end of class, Professor Irons flipped on the light and handed out papers to the students in the front of each row to pass back. I scanned the paper as he explained our assignment. "By next Friday, view one of the Holocaust films I've put on reserve in the media viewing room at the library. Complete the assignment I've just distributed and submit it through the university portal."

"Can we get the films online?" a girl up front asked.

"Sorry, we're kicking it old-school with VHS tapes," Professor Irons said with a coy grin. "Can you believe the library still has VHS players? They're called VCRs."

The class broke into laughter.

"These films are cinematic classics, and if you were to find them on the World Wide Web, they're only on VHS which I'm guessing none of you have the ability to play on your modern technology," he continued with amusement in his eyes. "I assure you, there are enough films to choose from that if you all end up at the library at the same time—which is unlikely since you'll be working with partners—you'd still have your choice of films."

Partners?

"There are six rows, five in each row," Professor Irons said. "I'm going to make this very easy on you. The first row by the door, turn to the person on your left."

My stomach dropped and I closed my eyes, knowing I was going to hate this project.

"Rows three and five do the same. Say hello to your partner for the term," Professor Irons said. "Be sure to exchange your digits or whatever it is you kids say today. And be sure this first assignment is complete for Friday."

The other students happily introduced themselves to their partners and exchanged numbers. I grabbed my things and stuffed them into my bag. "You know where to find me," I muttered as I stood and hurried out of the room without even looking at my damn partner.

CHAPTER FIVE

I stayed in my room most of the day Saturday doing homework and watching movies while Chantel was off preparing for more rush events. She didn't come home that night, likely spending quality time with Chase.

I ate breakfast with Valerie Sunday morning then returned to my room where I remained in yoga pants and a T-shirt for the entire day watching football, something my dad and I did religiously. He didn't get the son he obviously would've liked to have, so I got to do all the guy things with him—and I wasn't complaining. I loved sports, especially football.

Just after seven, there was a knock at my door. I crawled off my bed and walked to it, pulling it open a crack.

Unexpectedly, the door pushed all the way open, causing me to stumble back. Chase pushed his way inside my room.

"Whoa," I said, spinning around to face him. "Chantel's not here."

"You know where to find me," he said, using my words on me.

"I…"

He crossed his arms and leaned his ass against my desk in low hung grey basketball shorts, a tight-fitting navy T-shirt, and a backpack on his back. "Well, here I am. So, grab your shit and let's go."

I crossed *my* arms. "I'm not going anywhere with you."

"It's my grade too, *partner.*"

I let out a shaky breath. No matter how much I hated this—and no matter how much the universe was working against me—*he'd* been the one who was rude. Not me. I wouldn't play his game. I was better than that.

I gave a sigh of resignation and walked to where he stood, stopping in front of him. "Move."

He didn't, his eyes now on my television. "Why are you watching football?"

I tilted my chin up. "Because I like it. Now move."

He still didn't budge, but something unfamiliar flashed in his eyes.

"I need my stuff," I explained, knowing we'd stand like that all night if he thought I was kicking him out.

He pushed off my desk with his signature glare and moved to the other side of the room. "You changing?"

I spun to look at him. "Oh, I'm sorry. Are yoga pants and a T-shirt not good enough for frat boy?"

His eyes narrowed. "I meant do you need me to step out so you can change."

"Oh." *Idiot.* I snatched my backpack off my chair and tucked my laptop inside. "Let's go."

He followed me out the door, closing it on his way out. We walked down the hallway in silence, two strangers—and enemies—trying to co-exist. I wasn't short, but he was a full foot taller than me and I felt the height difference as we made it down the three flights of stairs and outside into the dark night. I hadn't explored the library yet, so I didn't even know where to head. Sensing my confusion, he began walking to the left of my dorm.

I kept pace with Chase's long strides. He said nothing, so I did the same as we crossed the nearly deserted campus to the library. Lights filtered through the windows of the glass exterior of the tall modern building—such a contrast to all the older buildings that surrounded the quad. Vast stone steps led up to the entrance to the library. When we reached the front door, he pulled it open and walked through, letting it practically close in my face. *Asshole.*

Maintaining my composure, I kept up with him as he walked through the lobby and right to the elevator at the far side. He jammed his finger into the button and we waited, the silence between us growing. The elevator chimed and the doors split apart. We stepped inside and Chase pressed the button for the sixth floor. The doors closed and the tension in the air could be cut with a knife. "Where's Chantel?" I finally asked.

"Not her keeper."

"She didn't come home last night," I said, looking for a reaction.

He gave none.

The elevator door opened, and we stepped out to a floor filled with wooden tables. Some were occupied by groups studying and working quietly. Others were devoid of bodies but covered with books and open laptops. I followed Chase to the right until we stopped outside a dark room with windows filling the front. One strip of tiny blue floor lights running the perimeter of the room gave off minimal light inside.

As we stepped inside, I glanced around at the cubicles with televisions on desks and comfy chairs in front of them strategically set up in different areas of the room.

Chase walked to the counter where a short girl in glasses stood. She spoke to a guy in front of us. "I'm sorry. But it looks like it's been taken out."

"What the fuck?" he growled at her. "I've got a paper due tomorrow." His voice grew louder and angrier. "What the hell am I supposed to do?"

In the dim light of the small desk lamp on her counter, we could see her inch back from the counter, clearly unsettled by this guy.

"Whoa," Chase said, getting in the guy's face. "I heard her say someone took it out."

The guy, though not as big as Chase, glared at him. "What?"

"I think you owe her an apology."

After a long staredown, the guy tore his eyes away from Chase and glanced to the girl. "My mistake." He turned and stormed out of the room.

"You good?" Chase asked the girl.

She nodded. "Thank you."

I blinked several times, trying to comprehend what I'd witnessed. Was Chase actually capable of kindness? Had he really just shown a sliver of humanity to this girl?

"He was a jerk," Chase assured her.

She nodded, still visibly shaken but trying to wear a brave face. "What can I do for you?" she asked.

"We need one of the movies Professor Irons put on reserve," he said.

"Which one?" she asked.

"You choose," he said, a light tone to his voice. "Though the shortest one would be appreciated."

Wait. Was that a dig at spending time with me?

She spun around and searched the shelves behind her for a movie. She pulled out a VHS tape and handed it to

Chase. "I leave at nine, so just return it to the returns basket when you're finished."

"You bet," he said, turning away from her and moving to one of the television cubicles. We had our pick since no one else was in the media room. He pulled out a chair at a corner cubicle with two chairs and dropped into it.

"That was a nice thing you just did," I said.

He said nothing.

Grrr. I lowered my bag to the floor and sat down beside him. "Do you know how to use a VCR?"

He shot me a sideways glare.

"It was a valid question."

The cold tone returned to his voice. "Do you think I live under a rock?"

"Well, I'd say you were definitely raised by wolves."

He ignored my dig and inserted the video.

I pulled the assignment out of my bag, reading over the requirements. We needed to cite each time the film depicted an event that mirrored modern society.

"What do we need to do?" he asked.

"*Oooooh.* Can you not read?"

"You can't help yourself, can you?" he said, pulling the assignment from his bag so he didn't need to depend on me for the information. "You've got a comeback for everything."

I scoffed. "And you have a rude comment for everything."

"Only when it comes to you."

I pressed my palm to my chest. "Should I feel honored?"

Annoyance flashed across his face, my refusal to concede to him clearly bothering him.

The black and white movie began on the screen, and we turned our attention to it.

My eyes struggled to adapt to the movie's lack of high definition. And, thirty minutes in, I found myself completely distracted. Between the boring movie and the eye strain, I couldn't focus. Then, there was also Chase's kindness toward that girl that kept popping into my mind. It was like my brain was trying to link the two Chase's together and having major difficulty. Who was he really? The nice guy who helped someone in need? Or, the cruel guy who didn't know how to smile?

The minutes ticked by. And soon, the stark realization that we were very alone in that dark media room hit me. His crisp woodsy cologne kept inching its way over to me, inhabiting each one of my breaths. Then, the vision of him barging into my room kept replaying in my mind. I wished the way he just commanded a room with his tall body and pronounced muscles hadn't made me visualize him doing very inappropriate things. But they had. *God dammit they had.*

The urge to look over at him began to rival that of me trying not to eat chocolate.

I was smarter than this.

I gave myself an internal tsk. Something was clearly wrong with me. Yes, he was good looking, with his perfectly styled dark hair and full lips. Yes, he showed he could be kind when he wanted to be. But, he was a complete freaking asshole the rest of the time.

And I hated him for it.

"How many do you have written?" he whispered.

I startled, as if he'd overheard my mind's ramblings. I took a second to pull my thoughts together, then glanced to my notebook. "Six."

"Six?"

"Do you have more?"

He shook his head.

I sighed. "The point of having a partner is to share information. We can compare our notes at the end."

He yanked my notebook from my hands.

"You're seriously the rudest guy I've ever met."

He held his palm to his chest. "Should I be honored?"

I pressed my lips together, hating that he used my own line on me—*again*. "You can have my answers, but we still need to write the paper together."

"I have something every day this week. This needs to get done tonight."

"We have class at eight," I said, noting it was nearing ten.

He handed me back my notebook. "Yeah, well, we need to get this done tonight. You better type fast."

Rude *and* bossy.

The film ended an hour later. As the credits rolled, I pulled out my laptop and opened a blank document.

"Just add me to the doc and we can do every other paragraph," he said.

"Fine. But let's brainstorm a direction and we'll type as we talk."

For the next two hours, we shared ideas, combined them, and shockingly composed a hell of a paper. Though I'd never say it out loud, Chase was a lot smarter than I expected.

"I'm not sure how they did things at your old school, but you need to submit essays through the university portal," he said.

"Done." I sent it off to the professor through the portal. "We had that in Maine, too."

He gathered his stuff. "Why'd you transfer here, anyway?"

Surprised by the personal question, I shrugged. "I wanted to be closer to home."

"Where's home?"

"Chantel didn't tell you?"

He shook his head as he slung his backpack over his back. "We don't do a whole lot of talking."

Of course, they didn't. "I'm from Cedarville. It's a small town about forty-five minutes from here."

He nodded.

The urge to ask where he was from came over me, but I refrained for fear of the evil Chase rearing his ugly head.

He pushed himself to his feet. "You ready?"

I gathered my bag as he ejected the movie and brought it back to the desk, dropping it in the returns box.

He met me at the door, surprising me by opening it and holding it for me. We journeyed through the now-deserted sixth floor toward the elevator. The elevator eventually arrived, and we stepped in, closed alone inside once again. I shuffled my feet, maintaining a comfortable distance between us. I hated that I could hear his steady breathing, and that damn cologne had followed me, taunting me with its freshness.

The elevator stopped on the main floor and the doors opened. Relieved to be free of the closed-in space, I walked toward the exit. We stepped outside and descended the steps together. "I'll see you in the morning," I said.

"Fuck that."

My brows shot up.

"You're not walking back to the dorms alone."

"I'm not?"

He shook his head, taking off in the direction of my dorm.

"I'm fine," I said, following after him. "I've got mace and a phone."

He stopped and spun toward me, anger brewing in his eyes. "What the hell is wrong with you?"

"Excuse me?"

"Do you make a habit of putting yourself in unsafe situations for a reason?"

"What are you talking about?"

"The scene at the frat house."

I threw my hands out to my sides. "The scene *you* made?"

He dragged his hands through his hair. "Stop trusting people you don't know. It's like you're hell-bent on throwing yourself into the lion's den."

My face scrunched. *Lion's den*? "What does that even mean?"

"It means you're too trusting."

I rolled my eyes. "Look, I'm not your girlfriend. I'm not even your friend. So, you need to stop telling me what to do."

He ground his teeth together and his jaw ticked.

"I'll take that ticking in your jaw as you understanding." I spun away from him and hurried toward the path that led to my dorm, leaving him in the dark. I didn't turn around, though the sound of snapping branches along the path gave me pause numerous times. But my need to prove I was strong urged me on.

When I finally spotted the light at the front of my dorm, I breathed a sigh of relief. I reached the door and scanned my I.D. card. The door unlocked and I stepped inside. Once I stood safely alone in the front foyer, I looked through the window out into the darkness. About fifty yards out, I spotted Chase turn away from the building and walk in the opposite direction.

He'd followed me home?

Why?

CHAPTER SIX

Chase didn't show up to History through Film the following morning. I wondered if he was avoiding me since our encounter the previous night ended so badly.

When he still wasn't there Wednesday, I began to get curious. Maybe it wasn't me. Maybe something else was going on with him. But if I asked Chantel, I'd be raising questions I didn't want to have to answer.

On Friday, when he still wasn't there, I could think of nothing else throughout Professor Irons' lecture. Our last conversation played through my mind. Why had he wanted to get the paper done so early? He'd blamed having something to do—likely fraternity rush stuff I assumed, but that wasn't happening at eight o'clock in the morning.

* * *

My legs bounced restlessly as Chantel joined Valerie and me for breakfast on Saturday morning for the first time ever. Our normally light conversation seemed forced and awkward with Chantel there.

"We're partying at Kappa Sigma tonight," Chantel said.

"I haven't seen Chase around lately," Valerie said.

My head whipped in Valerie's direction. She noticed he'd been missing too? I hadn't mentioned it to her. *Hell.* I hadn't mentioned anything about him to anyone.

"Why would you?" Chantel snapped at her, making me thankful I hadn't been the one to bring it up.

Valerie's eyes grew distant and her shoulders sagged.

A sinking feeling formed in my stomach. I hated the way Chantel spoke to Valerie.

It was as if no one had the guts to speak up to her. I guess I understood their fear. Her sugar-sweet personality definitely had the tendency to switch like lightning. No wonder why she had a thing for Chase. His split personality mirrored hers.

* * *

"You're coming, right?" Chantel asked as she returned from her shower later that night.

"Nah. I'm just gonna stay in tonight," I said, knowing I'd been banned from Kappa Sigma. And, since I hadn't seen Chase since Sunday night's incident, running into him when drinks were flowing freely seemed like a bad idea.

She shrugged. "Suit yourself."

Thirty minutes later, there was a knock on the door. "Can you get that?" Chantel asked as she curled her hair in the closet mirror.

I rolled off my bed and pulled open the door. A group of sorority girls filed in, filling the room. Laughter and chatter overtook our once quiet space, and girls drinking from red cups made themselves comfortable on my bed—where I'd been laying.

"Why aren't you dressed?" Valerie's roommate Tina asked me.

I leaned against my desk. "I'm staying in tonight."

"Why?" another girl asked as if I'd lost my mind.

Valerie leaned against the desk beside me. "Please come."

"I'm just not feeling it. Next time."

Her lips twisted regrettably. I was starting to see she liked having me around. I'd become a sort of buffer between her and the others. "Text if you change your mind."

I nodded, feeling guilty for not being there for her.

Within minutes, the girls were up and heading out. Valerie looked over her shoulder. "You sure?"

I nodded. "Have fun."

Once the room had emptied out and silence filled the small space again, I switched on the television and chose a movie to stream. I climbed under my blankets and settled in, watching my movie in peace. Once it ended, I contemplated beginning a new one.

My phone pinged beside me, pulling my attention to it. I grabbed it and checked the screen. It came from an unknown caller. **Didn't take you for someone who followed orders.**

I typed a reply. **Who is this?**

The text appeared almost immediately. **How many people give you orders?**

My heart rate quickened. I knew there was only one person who'd send that text. And by now, he would've realized I followed that order and hadn't shown up with the others. I stared at my screen, waiting for another text. But another one didn't come.

What had his text meant? Was he challenging me? Taunting me? Laughing at me?

For a minute, I considered going to the party. But as much as staying away from Kappa Sigma had given Chase what he wanted, showing up would've been doing the same. He was making this a challenge. He was testing me. But why?

And, why had he followed me home from the library? Was he *really* just worried about my safety?

I checked the time. Eleven-fifteen.

Hmmm.

I rolled off my bed and moved to my closet, looking for something to wear—*if* I decided to go.

I could just show my face, check on Valerie, then get the hell out to prove I did what I wanted? Or, I could just stay home and forget the text ever came.

Dammit.

I grabbed a pair of jeans from the stack on the top shelf of the closet and a sleeveless black shirt with sparkles along the bottom and pulled them on. For someone who didn't want me walking on campus alone, he had to know he was forcing my hand and making me do it.

After pulling my hair up into a high ponytail, I stepped outside. For a Saturday night, the campus was dead. I looked around, knowing I was about to do something incredibly stupid.

A car idled by the curb with a man in the driver's seat. "Sophia?" he called through the open passenger window.

You've got to be kidding me.

I ducked my head to speak to him. "Who's asking?"

"Your Uber driver."

"I didn't order an Uber," I challenged.

"Your friend did."

My friend? *Right.* "Where are you supposed to take me?"

"Kappa Sigma."

I scoffed. "Of course you are."

Was this his idea of an olive branch? Or, was I just that predictable?

I pulled the door open and slipped into the backseat of the car, cursing every move I made. As we drove, I stared out the window at the deserted campus, wondering why I was doing this. Was I proving I didn't take orders? Or was I doing the complete opposite and proving I did?

The car stopped in front of Kappa Sigma a few minutes later. Light poured out of the windows. I pushed open the car door and stepped out, glancing back at my driver. "Thanks."

I made my way up the sidewalk to the pounding of bass beneath my feet, hating every step I took. I steered clear of stupidity. So why was I there?

I climbed the front steps and paused. I didn't need to do this. I had nothing to prove.

I turned back around.

"Where are you going?" a deep voice asked.

I inhaled sharply. My eyes shifted to the side of the front porch where the voice had come from. Ryan sat there, his phone in his hand. A relieved breath rushed out of me. "You scared me."

He laughed. "Sorry. You just looked unsure if you wanted to go in or leave."

I walked over and sat beside him on a glider chair. "Why are you all alone out here?"

He shrugged. "Sometimes it gets to be too much in there."

"I bet."

We sat in silence for a long time. Crickets chirped in the dark and a passing car sped by.

"Thanks for making me feel welcome last time I was here," I said.

"I could tell you were uncomfortable." He looked to me and grinned. "And it was clear you weren't like the Alpha Phis. They can be a little…"

"Extra?"

He chuckled. "Intimidating."

I shrugged. "I think they're all just trying to figure out where they fit in. Isn't that what we're all just trying to do, really?"

He thought about it for a minute, then nodded. "I think you're right."

I bumped him with my shoulder. "I'm always right. You best remember that."

He laughed as he pushed himself to his feet. He turned to me and extended his hand. "Come on, Maine. Let's go fit in."

I smiled as I grabbed hold of his hand and walked inside the crowded house. Music echoed from below as we made our way through the packed hallway toward the basement door. He didn't release my hand as he led me downstairs. We stopped on the second to last step, taking in the dance floor. Bodies jumped around to the party anthem pounding through the big speakers on the bar. I spotted Valerie, who waved excitedly, clearly happy I'd changed my mind. If only she knew why.

The dance music suddenly switched to a slow song. Those without partners abandoned the dance floor and moved to the side of the room. As the floor cleared leaving only couples, my eyes collided with Chase's. He swayed with Chantel, but his blue eyes were locked on mine. It was uncomfortable to maintain eye contact with someone for such a long time. But, I wouldn't look away. He'd gone to great lengths to get me there. Not only did I want to know why, but I wanted to see what he planned to do.

"Come on," Ryan said, pulling me onto the dance floor, still holding my hand.

Chase's eyes dropped to our hands, watching us as we moved to the opposite side of the dance floor.

Ryan turned to me and pulled me in to him. "See, Maine? We're fitting in."

I draped my arms over Ryan's shoulders and only then did I pull my attention from Chase. My mind whirled and my heart did crazy flips inside my chest. It was completely irrational to feel this way. I knew that. But I couldn't control it. Once Ryan turned us half a rotation, I could see across the room and Chase's eyes were again locked on mine.

My stomach dipped in a way I hated. Chase's gaze elicited so many unwanted feelings. There was something to be said for having a staring contest with a hot guy who seemed hell-bent on proving he was tougher than me. I just wished his eyes weren't so damn hypnotic.

Then, as if it were happening in slow motion, he broke eye contact. He lifted his hands and cupped Chantel's cheeks. He leaned in and kissed her—all lips and tongue—for the entire room to see.

I heard distant catcalls. People around them smiled. And a guy yelled, "Get a room."

My stomach roiled, embarrassment grasping hold of my body. I'd been played. I'd walked right into the lion's den.

Dammit.

I tore my attention away from the uncomfortable scene, cursing my own stupidity. What the hell was I doing there? I walked right into his screwed-up world, and I wanted no part of it. I stepped away from Ryan. "Thanks for the dance, but I've gotta go."

Without giving him a chance to respond, I ducked through the people surrounding the dance floor, climbed the stairs, and rushed through the crowded hallway. Once I stepped outside, I inhaled deeply, hating myself for even showing up.

I *knew* better.

I looked out at the road, noticing my Uber still sitting at the curb.

What the hell?

I walked over to it, ducking my head once again to speak to the driver through the open window. "Why are you still here?"

"I was told to wait."

I closed my eyes and a humorless laugh cut out of me like a shard of broken glass.

Mission accomplished.

As much as I prided myself on being a strong independent woman, in that moment, I was nothing but a fool.

CHAPTER SEVEN

I was watching football and doing homework Sunday night when I heard the click of my door unlocking.

Chantel walked in wearing what appeared to be a guy's shirt since it hung to her knees, and the jeans she'd worn to the party last night. I wondered if Chase had kept her with him to drive the point home that they were together, and I'd been a toy used solely for his amusement.

"Hi," she said, as she entered the room and went right to her dresser to grab clothes. "Heard you stopped by the party last night."

My stomach dropped. "Oh, I—"

"Ryan said you didn't stay long."

I released a quiet breath. "Yeah. I wasn't feeling too good."

She nodded as she moved to the closet and picked up her toiletries. "Are you feeling better now?"

I nodded, pretending to write something important in my notebook so she'd stop asking questions.

She took the hint and moved to the door. "I'm going to shower."

Once she stepped into the hallway, I released another breath. Why did I feel so guilty? I hadn't done anything wrong. Her hook-up buddy had reached out to me. He'd gone out of his way to get me to his party. Gone out of his way to prove to me that he and Chantel were solid.

I turned off the television, put my books away, set the alarm on my phone, and settled into bed, hoping to be asleep by the time Chantel returned.

I heard the door unlock a little while later, opening and closing quietly.

"Sophia?" Chantel whispered.

I contemplated answering, but my guilt and embarrassment over the previous night, wouldn't allow it.

"Stay away from Chase," she whispered.

I pinched my eyes together tightly, wishing I could crawl into a hole and disappear.

"He doesn't want you."

The door opened and closed again, and silence filled the room.

Had she left?

Did she just want me to think she'd left?

I didn't dare move. Didn't dare speak.

Why did she think I wanted Chase?

Had he said something?

Had she actually seen me there and my reaction to their PDA?

Oh, hell.

* * *

I awoke to the sound of my alarm the next morning. I silenced it and glanced to Chantel's side of the room, relieved to see that her bed was still made. I hopped out of bed, pulled on jeans and a vintage Nirvana T-shirt, grabbed my backpack, and ducked out of my room. My relief would undoubtedly be short-lived since Chase was in my first class.

I grabbed a coffee on my way to class, needing the caffeine more than I realized, and trekked toward the history building. Of course, I arrived before most, taking my seat in the back.

I sensed Chase before I heard him. The hair on the back of my neck stood on end as he slipped into the seat beside me. My body tensed, but there was no way in hell I'd let him see that he fazed me.

"Have fun Saturday night?" he asked.

Instead of meeting his gaze, I reached into my bag and pulled out my laptop. "Nope. It was pretty uneventful."

He scoffed. "I think your roommate would disagree."

Inwardly, I groaned, the vision of the two of them turning my stomach as it had that night.

"You into Ryan?" he asked.

Slowly, I swung my head toward him. "Are we seriously going to do this right now?"

"Do what?"

My eyes narrowed, ready to tell him what I thought of his little stunt Saturday night.

"Mr. Reed and Ms. Galloway," Professor Irons called as he stepped into the classroom, dropping his briefcase loudly onto the front desk.

Our attention shot to him.

"I've yet to receive your paper. Was there a problem meeting?"

I felt the color drain from my face and Chase's steely gaze move to me. "I submitted it through the portal last Sunday."

Professor Irons typed into his computer, staring intently into the screen. "It's not here."

"You said you knew how to do it," Chase gritted out beside me.

I glared at him. "I do." I opened the folder on my computer where the essay was saved and shared it once again through the portal. "I just sent it again," I explained to the professor as I waited with bated breath.

"Got it," he said, before glancing up at us. "But I'm deducting credit since it's late."

"What the fuck," Chase muttered.

"Professor, I can show you the time of our last edit. I'm new to Crestwood. I thought I knew how to use the portal, but I guess I missed a step."

"Sorry, Ms. Galloway. Deadlines are deadlines."

The sinking feeling in the pit of my stomach grew as I sat there stewing. I knew how to use the portal. I knew how to upload a God damned paper. And I *did* upload it. What the hell happened?

After a painstakingly long discussion on the historical accuracy of the roaring '20s as depicted in film—not to mention attempting to avoid Chase's angry stare for an hour straight, Professor Irons dismissed us.

I packed my notebook and laptop into my bag and, without giving Chase a chance to ream me out, I hurried out of class. Once outside and moving further away from the history building, I expected the pit in my stomach to dissipate, but if anything, it grew.

Things were spiraling out of my control. I thought moving back to Texas would change things for me. I just hadn't thought they'd change for the worse.

"Sophia!"

I tensed, the sound of my name on his lips like fingernails to a chalkboard. I quickened my pace, not in the mood to be reprimanded yet again.

"Stop, God dammit!" Chase growled, stepping ahead of me quickly so I had to stop.

"What?"

"I should be asking you the same question."

"I submitted that paper last Sunday the same way I submitted it today."

He cocked his head, disbelieving.

"For all I know, *you* went in and removed it. You're the only other person, besides Professor Irons, who had access to it and could've done it."

"Why would I do that?"

I scoffed. "*Seriously?* You sent an Uber Saturday night so I could watch you make out with Chantel."

His eyes tightened.

"You could've saved me the time and just sent the live stream I'm sure you've got set up."

His brows pinched together. "I didn't send an Uber."

I cocked my head to the side.

"I seriously have no idea what you're talking about." The bewildered look in his eyes couldn't be faked. He wasn't kidding.

A cold chill scampered up my spine. "But you texted me."

"So?"

"So? Then there was an Uber outside my dorm, and the driver said my friend sent it to bring me to *your* frat."

"I'm not your friend," he countered.

The twinge in my stomach gave me pause. What was wrong with me? He was right. We weren't friends.

"And why would you get in a stranger's car in the first place?" he asked.

"I thought…"

A sarcastic laugh escaped him. "You thought I wanted you at the party that bad I'd send a car for you?"

A blush crept up my neck and into my cheeks. When he said it like that, I felt so stupid.

"And you came," he said, confused. "Why?"

I tipped up my chin. "I don't back down from a challenge. When I'm pushed, I always push back." I swung around and hurried away from him. I was embarrassed and hurt and confused.

If he hadn't wanted me at the party, why had he texted me? Why, when I arrived, had he stared at me the entire time? And, if he hadn't sent the Uber to pick me up, who had?

CHAPTER EIGHT

The next day in Art History, I slouched down in my seat in the lecture hall. I hadn't seen Chase since the embarrassing run-in after class yesterday and planned to avoid him at all costs.

"Are we gonna talk about you getting into an Uber you didn't call for?" Chase asked from behind me.

Dammit. I closed my eyes, pinching them tight for a long moment.

"Just pointing out how yet again you put yourself in harm's way."

I twisted in my seat to find him leaned forward in the seat behind me. "You're in someone else's seat."

Exasperation clutched hold of his face as he shook his head. "Getting into a car that you've been *told* is an Uber. That you've been *told* is from a friend. That you've been *told* is taking you to a frat—is fucking dangerous."

I scrunched my nose. "Why do you care?"

"Because you're oblivious."

"I'm not the one who forgot where my seat was." I cocked my head. "Do these lapses in memory happen often for you?"

He growled, sitting back in his new seat and crossing his arms.

I smiled, laying on the sarcasm. "You know, I'm starting to totally see what Chantel sees in you."

His lips slipped into a cocky grin that would've melted my panties had it not belonged to a complete asshole. "Are you referring to my pretty eyes or hot body?"

"Oh, no," I said, laying on the sugar sweetness thicker. "It's your unwavering charm. It just exudes from every part of you. You're like a ray of sunshine. Like the pot of gold at the end of a rainbow. Like snow falling on Christmas morning."

His smug grin remained firmly in place. "What can I say?"

"Nothing." The phony smile slipped off my face. "That's your problem. As soon as you open your mouth, you suck." I twisted back around and tried to ignore the fact that he had decided to now sit behind me—likely shooting daggers at the back of my head during the entire lecture.

At the end of class, I contemplated my next move as I gathered my things. Contemplated ignoring Chase. Contemplated making one more comment. But before I could carry out any move, he disappeared.

* * *

"So, what happened to you Saturday night?" Valerie asked over dinner that night. She'd had sorority stuff the last three nights, so we hadn't eaten together—hence her asking me about the party the first chance she got.

"What do you mean?" I asked, pushing my fork into my chocolate cake.

She popped the fry into her mouth. "One minute you were there, the next you were gone."

I shrugged. "I thought I wanted to be there."

"Something changed your mind?"

I nodded as I ate my cake, hoping she'd let my response go without question.

"Did it have something to do with Chase?" she asked.

My guilty eyes widened. "Why would you say that?"

"Oh, I don't know. Maybe because I saw him *staring* at you."

I averted my gaze.

"And, *you* were staring at him," she said.

I looked back to her. "It was a misunderstanding."

"Do tell."

"We have some classes together."

She leaned closer, her chin now resting in her palm. "Oh, I like where this is going."

"No," I cut her off. "This isn't going anywhere."

"I don't understand. He's not technically dating Chantel."

"You can't tell her we had this conversation," I said, suddenly nervous whatever I said could get back to Chantel.

Valerie popped another fry into her mouth. "Oh, I'm no fool. It would be both our funerals."

"It's not even like that. I just thought he was challenging me."

Her brows furrowed. "Challenging you?"

I sighed. "We didn't get off on the right foot. At that very first party, the first weekend, he told me not to come back to the frat house."

Her mouth hung open. "Why?"

I shrugged. "Some stupid reason about putting myself in bad situations. Whatever the case, I thought he was challenging me to show up."

"Then he made out with Chantel in the middle of the dance floor once you got there?"

"You saw that?" I asked.

"Everyone saw that."

"Yeah, but they hook up," I said, confused.

She lifted a shoulder. "So, she says."

"What is it with you and Chantel?"

Her face fell slack. "What do you mean?"

"You don't seem like you like her."

She scoffed. "No one likes her. We *tolerate* her."

"Why?"

"Because we're sisters. But, she's a lot. And her mood swings are impossible to keep up with."

"I feel the same way about Chase."

"What made you think he wanted you at the party?"

I closed my eyes, embarrassed to admit it. "I thought he got me an Uber."

She gasped.

My eyes locked on hers, scared to ask but needing to know. "What?"

"*I* sent the Uber," she admitted.

"*You?*"

"We usually hire one for the night to bring us back and forth from our sorority house—or the dorms now— whenever we're ready to go. I hoped you'd change your mind about the party, so I told him to head back and wait in case you did."

I buried my face into my palms feeling like a complete and utter fool.

"I'm so sorry, Sophia."

"I'm such an idiot."

CHAPTER NINE

"Go skydiving," Chantel said as I walked into our dorm room after my afternoon classes the next day. She'd been even busier than Valerie, so I'd seen her even less than Val.

I figured she was on the phone, so I closed the door behind me quietly. But when I turned, I found her sitting on my bed with *my jar*. "What are you doing with that?"

She held up the mason jar I kept hidden under my bed. "Oh, this?" she asked innocently, though she was clearly far from innocent. "I just found it."

"Under my bed?"

"This is *our* room. I thought we share things?"

With heat rising into my cheeks, I walked toward her with my hand outstretched. "May I have that back please?"

Ignoring my request, she pulled another small piece of paper from inside the jar and unfolded it.

My pulse slammed hard against my skin. "*Chantel?*"

"Visit five new states," she read. "Boring." She tossed the paper to the side and pulled out another piece and unfolded it.

I reached for my jar but she pulled it back.

"Lose my virginity." Her eyes instantly jumping to mine. "You're a virgin?"

I grabbed the jar from her hand. "This is not yours."

"But we're friends," she said. "Aren't we?"

"A friend doesn't invade someone else's privacy." I grabbed the papers she'd opened and shoved them back into my jar. With a now shaky hand, I closed the lid and held my jar tightly to my chest.

"You're clearly embarrassed," she said, offhandedly. "Don't take it out on me."

My eyes widened, appalled by her nerve. "You're the one who snooped through my personal things. How would you feel if I did that to you?"

She looked me dead in the eyes. "What's mine is yours." Her words, mixed with her warning the other night, told me what this was really about.

With my jar in hand, I grabbed my backpack and yanked open the door. Without another word, I let the door slam behind me. I hurried down the hallway and away from my room, my heart racing the whole time.

Had she wanted me to find her looking through my jar?

Was she sending a message that she could do what she wanted when she wanted to?

I climbed the stairs to Valerie's room and knocked on the door. She opened it, smiling once she found me standing there. "Hi."

Tina was in the room, so I stepped back, not wanting to go inside.

"What's wrong?" Valerie asked, noting the indecision on my face.

"Can we go somewhere and talk?"

She slipped out of her room and closed the door. "What did Chantel do?"

I rolled my eyes. "It's so stupid."

"Come on," Valerie said, leading me to the stairwell. I followed her down to the first floor and out the back exit of the dorm to the small pond. "She won't come out here."

We started walking around the walking path surrounding the pond and made our way halfway before sitting on the first wooden bench we came to. I pulled off my backpack and placed it and the jar down beside me. Still feeling riled up, I gazed out at the pond watching two swans floating by side by side.

Valarie's eyes cut to mine. "You gonna tell me what Chantel did? I assume it has something to do with that jar."

"I walked in on her going through it."

"And it's something important to you?"

I nodded.

She didn't pry—like a true friend who knew I'd open up when I was ready. Even though we'd only known each other for a short time, I knew Valerie *was* a true friend. She was someone I could talk to and rely on.

"It's just a bucket list of things I want to do before graduating. But some of them are really personal."

"Like getting nipple rings?" Valerie bumped me with her arm, letting me know she was joking.

I laughed. "Something like that."

"Why do you think she did it?" she asked.

I shrugged, though I was fairly certain I knew.

"So, what are you gonna do about it?"

"I'm not sure. I'm so mad right now that she even did it."

"You should bleach one of her favorite shirts. Or, wait, cut her hair while she's asleep. Or, better yet—"

"You're starting to scare me."

We shared a laugh. And, as much as I appreciated her trying to make me laugh and lighten the mood, I still had no idea what I was really going to do about this problem with Chantel.

"Was Chantel like this last year?" I asked. "Or do you think she's just acting out because your house got shut down?"

"She's definitely gotten worse."

"Do you think Sydney Lane's death changed her?"

Valerie's eyes shot to mine. "What?"

"No one's mentioned Sydney. Not you, not Chantel, not anyone. But I'm sure losing her last year must've been difficult on all of you."

Valerie closed her eyes, pained by my words. "She was a great person," she whispered.

"There are a lot of great people who struggle with mental illness," I said.

She didn't look at me, though I could see her eyes opened and focused on her shoes. "Her family doesn't believe she struggled with any illness."

"That's why they're having it investigated?"

She nodded.

"What do you think?"

She shrugged. "They'd know their daughter better than anyone." Valerie pushed herself to her feet. "We should probably head back now."

"Oh," I said, realizing I'd made Valerie uncomfortable and she was done answering questions about her dead sorority sister. I grabbed my backpack and jar and stood, following her back to the dorm in silence. "You wanna get dinner?" I asked when we neared the back door of the building. "I really don't want to go back to my room yet."

Her mouth twisted as she considered my question. "I'm not really hungry."

"Oh." *What the hell? She was always hungry.* "Okay. I guess I'll just…see you tomorrow."

She nodded before walking back inside the dorm.

I didn't feel like eating alone in the crowded dining hall, but there was no way I could go back to my room feeling as unsettled as I did in that moment. Chantel pissed me off, and I needed space.

CHAPTER TEN

I ended up at the campus coffee house, taking a spot at the back corner table. The place was dead save for a few scattered people seated alone. I didn't bother popping in my earbuds, opting to eat my bagel sandwich and drink my coffee to the natural sounds of the whistling milk steamer and random orders being called.

Once I finished eating, I released the lid on the mason jar and pulled out the papers Chantel had so carelessly opened. I folded them back into the smaller squares they'd been in since I'd written each wish.

Had I overreacted? Did some people just not understand boundaries? Or, had she purposely done it to get a rise out of me? To punish me for—

The chair across from me scraped loudly back, and Chase dropped into it.

I said nothing, in no mood to banter with him right now. I closed my jar and pulled it closer to me.

"What's that?"

"Your girlfriend didn't already tell you?" I snapped.

His blank stare told me she probably hadn't.

"Never mind."

"You don't like her, huh?"

I lifted my coffee to my lips. "Not today."

He crossed his arms and leaned back in his chair. "What'd she do?"

"I don't feel like talking about it." I sipped my coffee and avoided his eyes, hoping he'd take the hint and leave.

He didn't. He remained in his chair staring at me from across the table.

"What?" I snapped. "Why are you still here?"

He glanced around the quiet coffee house. "Can't a guy get a cup of coffee?"

My eyes landed purposely on the empty space in front of him on the table.

"Chase the Great!" the barista called.

Chase smirked, and my eyes couldn't roll far enough back in my head. He stood and grabbed his coffee. I expected him to take off, leaving me to wallow in my anger, but he returned to my table, making himself comfortable in his chair.

"So, what's in the jar?" he asked.

"None of your business."

"Is it why you're mad at Chantel?"

I drank my coffee so I didn't have to answer him.

"You're different than she is. I think that's why you two won't be friends."

"We won't?"

He shook his head. "She needs people she can walk all over. People who obey her. You're not like that."

I wrinkled my nose. "Was that some kind of twisted compliment?"

"Oh, don't go getting crazy now."

I snickered.

So did he.

I tapped my hand on the top of my jar. "My bucket list is inside."

He examined the folded papers through the glass jar. "Looks like a lot of things you plan to do. You think you can do them all?"

I shrugged. "It would be a pity not to try."

His eyes lifted to mine and something I'd never seen before flittered across his face. Admiration, maybe. "Tell me something in that jar."

"Why?"

"Because now I'm curious," he dead-panned.

I contemplated his request. As much as he rubbed me the wrong way every time we spoke, we were partners for the semester. We would be spending more time together. What was the worst that could come from opening up a tiny bit? "I want to drive in a convertible along the coast."

His head hitched back. "That's it?"

"What were you expecting?"

He shrugged his big shoulders. "I don't know. Something crazy, like skydiving."

"That's in there too."

"Why a convertible?"

"Why not? I've never been in one. And I love the ocean. I just thought it would be an amazing experience."

"You need to aim higher."

My brows hitched up. "I do?"

"That jar's filled with wishes. And, you seem like a determined person. Why not aim for the stars?"

I said nothing as I stared back at him, more confused than ever before about who the real Chase Reed was. A frat boy with a chip on his shoulder? A protector of meek girls in libraries? A deep guy offering advice in a coffee shop? Satan?

"What?" he asked, subtle dimples digging in beside his lips.

I shook my head, smart enough not to tell him how confusing I found him to be.

He lifted his coffee cup and tipped it back like it wasn't piping hot.

"You disappeared."

He dodged my eyes, his latching on to something outside the window in the distance. "I do that sometimes."

"You do?"

He nodded.

I tucked one of my waves behind my ear, stalling so not to appear too interested. "Where do you go?"

"Just got things to take care of."

"You got a secret baby or something?"

Laughter burst out of him, a sound so unfamiliar but so smooth it hit places deep inside me I hadn't expected. "No. Not even close."

I smiled, grabbing my jar with both hands, like a safety net. Because any minute now, he could resort to his mean self and I'd need it.

He looked back to my jar. "What else is in there?"

I tipped my head to the side. "Do you really care?"

He shrugged.

"I want to be the reason someone else does something amazing."

"Amazing is ambiguous. How will you know if you succeed?"

I smiled. "I'll know."

Chase's lips twitched in the corners, but before he would allow himself to smile more than once in a conversation, he pushed his chair back and stood. "I'll tell Chantel to play nice."

"Oh, no you won't."

His eyes narrowed, caught off guard by my objection.

"I can handle her."

A harsh, humorless laugh escaped his throat.

"Well, tell me then. How would that conversation go? Hey, Chantel. I had coffee with Sophia and she told me you went through her stuff—"

"She went through your stuff?" he asked.

I closed my eyes, cursing my big mouth.

"She went through your jar," he said, the puzzle pieces falling into place.

"As I was saying," I said, trying to distract his attention from what I'd just divulged. "Bringing up the fact that we've spent any time together, regardless of how innocent it's been, seems like a horrendous idea—for both of us."

"I'm not scared of her," he assured me, before turning and walking in no hurry toward the door.

The girl seated by the door working on her laptop peeked up as he passed, staring at him as he walked out.

I understood the inclination to look at him. Too bad he had a split personality and you just never knew who you were going to get.

* * *

I unlocked the door to my room. I pause with my hand wrapped around the doorknob as my lungs expanded on a long, deep breath, preparing myself to face Chantel. I pushed open the door, only to find the room empty. I exhaled, more relieved than I expected to be. I hated conflict, but she'd started this, and I wasn't sure it was something we could come back from. I couldn't trust her now.

And down deep, I wasn't even sure I liked her.

I went to my closet and pulled out an old pair of jeans I never wore. I rolled my jar inside the jeans and buried them in the back of my closet. If she planned to snoop again, I wasn't making it easy on her.

CHAPTER ELEVEN

I walked toward my dorm after my Thursday classes, really hoping Chantel wasn't there. We'd managed not to cross paths since yesterday when she'd gone through my jar, and I hoped to keep it that way. I knew she was leaving for the weekend for her cousin's wedding, and I really hoped she'd left early.

The cloudy sky sent a cool breeze whipping through the path I took back to the dorm. I hugged my arms around myself, thankful I'd worn my pink hoodie. I'd forgotten how inconsistent September weather could be.

I stepped off the path onto the sidewalk across the street from my dorm. An older woman, standing there staring up at the top floor, grabbed my attention.

I stopped, wondering what she was doing. Was she waiting for someone to come down to let her into the building?

When minutes passed and she still hadn't moved, I approached her. "Are you waiting for someone?"

Her eyes moved to mine. That's when I noticed she'd been crying.

An ominous shiver rushed up my spine. "Oh, my goodness. Are you all right?"

She shook her head.

My Lifetime movie senses kicked in. "Is there someone I can call for you?"

She shook her head again.

A bouquet of flowers lay beside her feet on the sidewalk. *Oh shit.*

"Would you like to sit down?" I motioned to the sidewalk and slowly sat down hoping she'd follow my lead.

She carefully lowered herself down beside me.

A heavy silence descended.

Another breeze whipped through sending goosebumps scampering up my legs. Our quiet was interrupted by students passing by, walking around us, and laughing and chatting with friends.

"Did you know my daughter Sydney?"

Though I had a sinking feeling it was Sydney's mom, my heart wilted as the truth hit me. I shook my head. "No, I'm sorry. I just transferred here."

"But you heard what happened?"

I nodded. "I'm so sorry for your loss. I can't even imagine your grief."

"It's torture."

Tears pricked my eyes.

"My husband would be furious if he knew I was here…I just needed…I just needed to see."

I nodded, understanding her need to seek closure after suffering such a tragic loss.

"She was the light of my life," she said.

A rogue tear escaped my eye and I quickly wiped it away. I couldn't imagine the grief she was feeling. I don't know what came over me, but I slipped my arm through hers.

Instantly, her body relaxed against me, as if she needed someone to comfort her.

We sat there for a long time.

"You're an angel," she said, turning to look at me. Her

puffy eyes assessed my face. "Sydney would've liked you."

I willed back the flood of tears threatening to fall and smiled. "I'm sure I would've liked her, too."

Tears glazed her eyes as she turned to look back at the top of the building. "My daughter would've never hurt herself."

Unsure what to say, I said nothing. Kids kept secrets from their parents, and no matter how well parents thought they knew their kids, they never knew everything.

"I just can't believe no one knows anything," she said softly.

"I'm sorry."

"Oh, honey. You've got nothing to be sorry for." The sun began to set and the breeze became cooler. She shivered, her light sun dress not enough to keep her warm. She unlocked her arm from mine. "I should get going. I just…I just needed this."

I pulled open my backpack and grabbed a pen and notebook. "I'm gonna give you my number." I scribbled down my name and number on a sheet of paper and tore it out of my notebook. "You call if you ever find yourself back here. I'll sit with you for as long as you need me to."

She took the paper from my hand and looked at it. "Sophia," she mused. "A beautiful name for a beautiful soul." She closed her hand over mine. "I think Sydney wanted us to meet."

"You think so?"

She nodded.

"Sophia?" Chantel called from the dorm entrance across the street.

My eyes shot to the door where Chantel stood, anger brewing in her eyes.

"What are you doing?" she asked.

Sydney's mother stood.

I followed her up. "This is Sydney's mom."

"We've met," Sydney's mother said through tight lips.

"How are you?" Chantel asked her.

"How do you think I am?" Sydney's mother's voice grew louder. "My daughter's dead and none of her so-called sisters know a damn thing."

"I'm sorry I can't help you," Chantel said. "I have class." She hurried away and Sydney's mother watched her go, a blank stare on her face. Her eyes cut to mine. "You know her?"

I nodded. "She's my roommate."

She closed her eyes, as if pained by the notion. "Watch that one. She's a sneak." Sydney's mother headed over to a BMW parked against the sidewalk. She pulled open the door and slipped inside. "It was nice to meet you, Sophia."

"You too."

She closed her car door and the engine purred to life. I watched as she gave the top of the building one last glance before pulling away.

I sat back down on the sidewalk, my legs shaking beneath me. I couldn't imagine that poor woman's grief. I also couldn't understand how no one knew *anything* about Sydney's death. *Or*, why Valerie and Chantel both reacted strangely to the mention of Sydney Lane.

If there *was* more to Sydney's story, like Sydney's mom believed, I hoped to God it came to light so she could finally have closure.

* * *

"What the hell was that?" Chantel asked as she stormed into our room that night.

Great. She was still here. I peeked up from my laptop. "Excuse me?"

"Don't play dumb. Sydney's mother. You didn't tell me you knew her."

"I don't. She was standing outside our dorm and something seemed wrong with her, so I talked to her. She's hurting. And she's looking for closure."

"Right. By closing *my* sorority."

My eyes widened. That was cold even for Chantel. "You've got to know she's grieving. She's not seeing clearly. I'm sure she doesn't want to hurt you guys. She just doesn't know what else to do."

"She needs to move on."

A cold chill rushed through me. Sydney was someone Chantel actually knew. I didn't even know Sydney, but the way her mother spoke of her made *me* cry. How could Chantel be so thoughtless?

But what did I expect? Chantel was self-absorbed. Some people were raised to think they were the center of the universe. I'd never be able to relate. I'd been taught by my parents—and Tim McGraw—to be humble and kind. Chantel just didn't possess those qualities.

Chantel and I were two totally different people. And, despite Chase's foresight, it was becoming abundantly clear that she and I would never be friends.

CHAPTER TWELVE

Saturday morning my phone buzzed, pulling me from a sound sleep. I reached over and grabbed it, hoping whoever was calling this early on a weekend had prepared themselves for my wrath. I checked the screen. *Unknown caller.* I dropped it back down, ignoring it.

But it continued to buzz.

I grabbed the phone again and lifted it to my ear. "Hello?"

"You've got ten minutes," a deep voice said.

"Who is this?"

"Get dressed, take care of whatever girls do in the morning, then come downstairs," Chase said.

I huffed. "Why?"

Dead air filled the line. I checked the screen and the bastard had hung up. *What was he up to?*

I crawled out of bed and moved to the window. I shielded my eyes from the bright sunlight as I checked the street in front of my dorm. No one was out there—no cars, no people, not even Chase.

Was this some kind of trick?

Was he trying to make some kind of point about me getting into the Uber I thought he'd sent?

Was he setting me up?

I closed my eyes and thought about what to do next. I could get dressed, go downstairs, and no one would be there. Or, I could stay put and go back to bed and pretend it never happened—like I should have done last weekend.

Grrr. I hated my curiosity.

I went to my closet, grabbed jeans, and a navy hoodie and pulled them on, then slid on my navy Converse. I ran to the bathroom to brush my teeth, then I secured my hair in a high ponytail. If this was a joke, I wasn't about to be caught in my pajamas with bedhead.

I grabbed my phone, tucked some money in my back pocket, and walked downstairs.

Damn him if this was a trick.

Damn him if he was going to show his split personality again.

Damn him for making me curious.

I reached the front door and inhaled deeply. *Please don't make me look stupid.* I pushed open the door. Air punched out of my lungs when I found Chase in a backward baseball cap leaned against a red convertible.

I blinked hard, making sure I wasn't having some kind of Jake from *Sixteen Candles* dream. "What are you doing?"

He smirked. "You *know* what I'm doing."

I swallowed my surprise. "Yeah, but why?"

"Can't a guy just do something nice?"

"A guy can. *You*…I'm not so sure."

He shook his head, a flicker of amusement lighting his eyes. "Get your ass in the car."

My feet stayed firmly planted to the sidewalk. "I'm serious. I don't understand."

"What's to understand? You get in Ubers with strangers. But you won't get in a car with me? You gotta see how messed up that is."

"You showing up here, when your girlfriend's away,

trying to grant me one of my bucket list wishes. You gotta see how messed up *that* is."

He twisted his hat around on his head and pulled it down low, molding the brim down. "For the love of God, she's not my girlfriend."

I crossed my arms. "Does *she* know that?"

"Yes."

I tipped my head to the side. "Does everyone else know that?"

"I don't give a fuck what anyone else thinks."

"Do you care what *I* think?"

He stared at me across the empty space, his blue eyes penetrating while his patience with me was clearly wearing thin. "Are you gonna get in the car or not?"

Oh, hell.

I walked slowly toward the car.

He opened the passenger door. My arm brushed his. Goosebumps broke out all over my skin as I slipped into the car, settling into the smooth leather seat.

Chase closed my door before circling the front and sliding into his seat. "Well, that was more difficult than I expected," he said as he pressed the button and the engine roared to life.

I cut my gaze to his. "Where'd you get the car?"

He pulled out onto the main street. "Don't worry about it."

I closed my eyes as we picked up speed, loving the free feeling of driving without windows or a roof. The warm September sun beat down and a breeze brushed against my cheeks as we moved through the streets. Once Chase turned onto the highway, I lifted my arms into the air and let the wind push them back, loving every minute of it.

"You having fun?" Chase asked.

I shrugged, not wanting him to be too proud of himself.

He smiled, and when he smiled like that—all teeth and dimples, I almost forgot about what a jerk he could be.

"You should do that more often," I said.

"What?"

"Smile."

He reached for the radio and turned it up, clearly not in the mood for conversation—or compliments.

I laughed to myself. Maybe he wasn't such a bad guy after all. Maybe the real Chase was the guy in the media room sticking up for that girl, and the guy who'd picked me up to make my bucket list wish come true.

Before long, we neared the coast. The briny air greeted us and laughing gulls flew overhead, their wings spread as they, too, eagerly neared the beach.

Chase lowered the music. "Get ready. You want to remember the moment your wish came true, don't you?"

Butterflies took flight in my stomach. But I feared those butterflies weren't because my wish was about to be granted. I feared it was because of the unlikely person granting that wish.

I absorbed the stunning view of the coast as he drove along it, slowing when no one was behind us on the road. I pulled out my phone and snapped pictures of the beautiful blue water with the puffy white clouds dangling in the air—a perfect backdrop to a perfect moment.

Chase hit his blinker and turned off the road into a dirt overlook. He parked the car and cut the engine. "Let me get your picture."

My brows furrowed.

"In the car. By the coast. Your wish."

Oh. Right. I handed him my phone and smiled as he snapped a few pictures, making sure to get me in the car in front of the ocean.

He handed me back my phone and circled around the car. But instead of getting back in, he leaned against the driver's side door and looked out at the ocean.

I gave him time, figuring he wanted to be alone. But once he still hadn't gotten back in after a few minutes, I stepped out of the car and walked over to him, leaning beside him against the car and staring out at the ocean. The waves crashed loudly, but I still couldn't ignore Chase's silence. He was never one to hold back his thoughts. But clearly, something was on his mind.

Maybe he regretted bringing me here. Maybe he thought I wanted to stay longer. Maybe he thought he was giving me what I wanted.

"Thanks for doing this for me," I said.

He didn't respond.

"I'm ready to head back now." I turned to go back to the passenger side of the car, but Chase reached out and grasped my arm. I stilled, not sure why he stopped me.

His hand slipped down my arm to my hand, and his fingers linked with mine.

I didn't dare speak. Move. Or even look at him.

"Don't let Ryan hold your hand again," he said.

I swallowed down my confusion. "Huh?"

"I don't want Ryan holding your hand anymore."

A million thoughts inundated my brain, none of which made any freaking sense. Why did he care if Ryan held my hand? Why did he think he could give me another order? Why was *he* currently holding my hand? "Then stop holding Chantel's hand," I countered, instantly wanting to eat my words. Why had I said that? Did I actually feel that way?

His eyes cut to mine, and a shiver skimmed down my spine. "Done."

We stayed like that, with our hands locked, for a long time, just watching the crashing waves. Both in our own heads. Both admitting feelings we probably would have rather not. What in the world was going on?

He eventually released my hand and turned to his door, pulling it open.

I walked back around to my side and got in.

I expected him to turn the car around in the overlook, but he didn't. He pulled back out onto the road and continued driving along the coast. I wanted to ask what he was thinking. If we were going to move forward as enemies or friends. But the fear of him turning on me, weighed heavy on my mind and caused my lips to remained zipped.

A short time later, Chase hit his blinker again and turned into a gravel parking lot where a food truck sat parked. Once he cut the engine, he hopped out of the car. I followed him to the food truck, where the menu was written on a chalkboard on the side of the truck. Everything contained shrimp. Good thing I liked seafood.

"See anything you'd like?" Chase asked.

"Shrimp tacos and fries."

He smiled before turning to the worker in the truck. "Make it two." He pulled out his money.

"I have money," I said, reaching for my back pocket.

Again, he reached out and grabbed my arm. This time his hand elicited tingles in the spot.

Dammit.

"You're not paying," he assured me.

I relaxed as he released my arm and paid the guy in the truck.

"Come on." He led me to a picnic table where we could wait for our food.

We sat on opposite sides and both stared out at the view.

"You're quiet," Chase said.

"I don't really know what to say," I admitted, my eyes still on the coast.

I could sense him nodding, as if he understood my sentiments.

"Did I do something to make you hate me when we first met?" My eyes moved from the ocean back to him.

He grabbed hold of the hat on his head and twisted it back around so it sat backward on his head. "I'm a complicated guy."

"Sounds like a load of BS."

He scoffed.

"Am I wrong?"

He shrugged.

"I think you're confused. Like you want to hate me, but you can't."

"Oh, I definitely can and have."

"See? That's what I don't get. What did I ever do to you?"

He pegged me with his eyes. "You came to Houston."

I flinched, his words blowing all clear thoughts from my head.

"I had my whole semester planned out. All the things I needed to accomplish," his eyes drifted from mine. "Then you showed up and threw everything on its head."

My heart began to race. What was he talking about? How had I done that?

"I don't want to like you, Sophia. But I do. And I don't know what to do with that." He glanced back to me. "And it's pissing me the hell off."

I pressed my lips together, not really sure what else to do in that moment. It confused me. It elated me. It messed with my head. There were two different versions of Chase. The protective, caring one. And the mean, bossy one. I just never knew who I'd get, and that pissed *me* off.

"So, I guess I picked you up today because I needed to see if I did something nice for you if you'd smile at me the way you smile at fucking Ryan."

My eyes widened. "Do you want me to smile at you like I smile at him?"

He shrug-nodded, such an unfamiliar vulnerability emanating from him.

"Then be nice to me. I'm not your enemy."

"It's not that easy."

"Try me," I said.

"I want to. But I can't."

"Sounds like the line you fed Chantel."

His brows drew in. "What line?"

"You don't have time to date anyone. But if you did, it would be her. You talk in circles."

He rolled his eyes.

"Don't roll your eyes. Those words are what keep her coming back to you. That or the sex."

He burst out laughing.

"What's so funny?"

"Order three!" the guy from the food truck called, interrupting our discussion.

Chase stood and walked over to the truck. I took that moment to release the breath I'd unknowingly been holding. What the hell was going on? He liked me? He doesn't want to, but he does? What world was he living in? What world was *I* living in?

He returned with our food, placing mine in front of me as he sat back down across from me.

We ate in silence for a bit, the crash of the waves the soundtrack to our meal.

He wiped his mouth with his napkin. "Why'd you choose Maine?"

"I wanted to get away from Texas."

His eyes drifted toward the water as if he were considering my answer. "You mean you wanted to get away from a guy?"

Though he wasn't looking at me, I shook my head. "I tore my ACL playing soccer my senior year in high school."

He looked back to me, surprise filling his eyes.

"I had a scholarship to play D1 soccer at the University of Texas that went out the window once I got hurt."

"That sucks."

I shrugged, not looking for sympathy. "I just got sick of all the looks of pity around town, so I made the decision to get far away. To try to forget the dream I lost. To start over."

"So, what happened that you're back?"

"It snowed. *A lot.*"

He smiled. "Why aren't you playing soccer now? Crestwood has a team."

"I'm just not into it anymore."

"Sounds like BS."

"Excuse me?"

"I seem to recall you telling me you don't back down from a challenge. When you're pushed, you always push back."

I chewed on my bottom lip, hating to have my own words thrown in my face. "Maybe I don't want to admit

I'll never be as good as I once was." *Wow. I'd never actually admitted that out loud.* Why of all people had I admitted it to Chase? "Why'd you choose Washington?" I asked, desperately needing to swing the conversation from me.

"How'd you know I transferred from Washington?"

"It's a small school. Doesn't everyone know everyone else's business?"

He shrugged, neither confirming nor denying. "I guess I just wanted to see other places."

"But now you're back?"

"I was needed back home."

"Your family needed you?" I asked.

"Something like that."

"Is home Houston?"

He nodded.

"I'm surprised you're in a frat."

"Why?"

"Just doesn't seem like your scene," I said.

"How do you know?"

I cocked my head. "You have to talk and be nice to people when you're in a frat."

He laughed, and the raspy sound was slowly becoming familiar to me.

I grabbed a fry and said, "Can I ask you something?"

"Do I have a choice?"

"No," I said, eating the fry.

He nodded.

"Did you ever meet Sydney Lane?"

Something unrecognizable flashed in his eyes. It was like the mention of her name put everyone at Crestwood on edge. He shook his head. "Why?"

"Her mom was on campus the other day."

His head flinched back. "She was?"

I nodded. "She was so sad."

"You spoke to her?"

"I could see she needed to talk to someone."

"Jesus Christ," he mumbled, as his eyes drifted out to the ocean.

"Chantel wasn't happy when she saw us together."

His eyes shot back to mine. "She saw you with Sydney Lane's mom?"

"She thought I already knew her."

"What'd Chantel say?" he asked, suddenly very interested.

"Just that Sydney's family was to blame for the sorority being closed."

"Sounds like Chantel," he said.

"Did she ever show any kind of sadness after it happened—you did hang out last year, right?"

He nodded. "Chantel's hard to read. Her emotions always contradict themselves." He lifted his chin toward my empty plate. "You done?"

My lips twisted regrettably, knowing that was his way of ending yet another conversation. "Yup."

He grabbed our plates and tossed them into a nearby garbage can. I followed him to the car. He pulled open the passenger door for me.

"Thanks," I said, slipping past him and into my seat.

He closed my door and made his way into the driver's seat. As soon as the car roared to life, he turned up the music and drove us back to campus. The volume left no room for conversation. And that was fine by me. The whole day had taken me by complete surprise, and we only risked spoiling it with words.

When he stopped in front of my dorm a little while later, he finally lowered the music.

I looked over at him. "Thanks for today. I had a surprisingly nice time."

He chuckled. "Nice, huh?"

"I'll see you Monday." I pushed open my door and stepped out.

"Soph," he said, the nickname rolling off his tongue smooth and sexy and rippling through my stomach like a swarm of bees.

I turned back to face him.

"I had a surprisingly nice time, too," he said.

Smiling, I closed the passenger door and walked to the entrance of my dorm. I didn't dare look back. Chase hadn't pulled away yet, and I really didn't want to see his pretty eyes staring back at me.

What in the world had just happened? Had we actually shared a nice day together? Had we come to an understanding? And if we had, what did it all mean?

Whatever it meant, I knew one thing for certain. I was so screwed.

CHAPTER THIRTEEN

I stood at the mirror, sweeping a little blush onto my cheeks before leaving for History through Film Monday morning. Normally, I ignored such primping, but I hadn't seen or heard from Chase since our trip Saturday, so…

"Hey," Chantel said as she stepped into our room, dropping her overnight bag by the door.

I plastered on a fake smile. "How was the wedding?"

"Good. I got back last night and spent the night at Chase's."

I steeled my features as jealously swirled in my stomach. I hated that it did. He and I were nothing to each other.

Chantel pegged me with her eyes. "He always knows how to welcome me home."

I bet he does. I grabbed my backpack off my chair a little rougher than I intended. "I've got class. I'll see you later." I walked out of the room and hurried down the hall, my mind whirling.

Did our day together mean nothing? Was it just another day to him? He said he didn't want to like me but he did. Was that just a line? Had I just read too much into him being jealous over Ryan?

Anger mixed with foolishness still coursed through me a few minutes later when I walked into class. Chase's seat was empty. *Good.* I didn't know what I'd say to him anyway.

Professor Irons walked into the classroom, speaking before he even placed down his briefcase. "I returned your papers in the portal. Did you all check your grades?"

I opened my laptop and checked the portal. The comment in the side margin of our paper read: *This would have been an A+. Next time get your work in on time!* B+

I groaned.

I felt Chase slip into his seat beside me. "What?" he asked.

Without looking at him, I turned my laptop so he could see the screen.

"Well, that sucks," he said. "I thought he'd forget it was late."

I scoffed.

"Your next paper is due Friday," Professor Irons began. "I think you're really going to enjoy the movies I selected for you this time."

"How many movies?" a guy in front asked.

Professor Irons' eyes lit up. "Two. And they're classics." He handed out the assignment to the people in front of each row and they passed it back to us.

As I reviewed the requirements, people around me groaned.

"Looks like I'm gonna have to carry us again," Chase said, attempting a joke.

I ignored his comment. Did he really think I was that stupid? Didn't he really think Chantel and I wouldn't cross paths once she left his room?

"Wanna get started tonight?" he asked.

"I'm sure you and Chantel will be meeting up like last night," I said, finally turning to look at him. *See? Not stupid.* "Wouldn't want to get in the way of that."

His eyes held mine. "Nope. No plans with anyone but you."

Professor Irons began his lecture, and I turned my attention to him. I spent the entire time ignoring Chase who spent the majority of class staring at me.

What did he want from me? If this was some kind of game, I wasn't playing.

Once Professor Irons dismissed us, I gathered my things and hurried out of class. I quickly made it down the hallway and stairwell, stepping outside the building where I could finally breathe.

Despite the breeze and chattering of students hurrying to their classes, I still heard the unwelcome sound of Chase's voice. "Sophia!"

I quickened my pace toward my next class, knowing I had nothing to say to him. We were nothing to each other. There was no reason for me to be mad. And there was no reason for him to explain. I just felt so stupid for believing he wasn't the guy I initially thought he was.

"Would you hold up?" Chase said, stepping in front of me and stopping me in my tracks.

I huffed. "What?"

"You never answered me about working on the project."

My eyebrows climbed. "That's what you wanted?"

He stared out at the bustling quad, avoiding my eyes. "Yeah."

He was such a liar. "I can't."

His eyes dropped to mine. "Why not?"

"I have plans."

His browns cinched in the middle. "With who?"

Hadn't thought that far ahead. "Ryan," I lied.

His eyes darkened, anger looming in them. "Why?"

"Because I like him. And I don't have to hate myself for liking him. It's easy. And he makes me smile." There, *asshole*. How do *you* like it?

He buried his hands in the front pockets of his jeans. "Are you hanging out at the house?"

"Don't even tell me I'm not welcome."

"That's not why I'm asking."

"Then, why? Will Chantel be there and you want us all to hang out together?"

Again, his eyes darted away from mine.

I stepped around him and took off to my next class, leaving him a distant memory—at least for the time being.

CHAPTER FOURTEEN

After dinner with Valerie, I returned to my room, thankful Chantel wasn't there—but wishing I wasn't curious where she was.

I pulled out my laptop and spent the next few hours completing my Art History assignment about the evolution of the female form. I based my support on various ancient works of art, and it turned out to be a fascinating assignment. Once I uploaded my essay to the portal—which I knew how to do, thank you very much—I tucked my laptop away and ducked out of the room to conduct my pre-bed routine. When I returned, I tucked my toiletries away in my closet.

There was a knock on the door. I stepped away from the closet and approached it. "Who is it?"

"Ryan."

Ryan? I pulled open the door. "Hey."

He held up a bag. "I brought you something."

I eyed it. "What is it?"

"Can I come in?"

"Do you have rope or handcuffs in that bag?"

His eyes widened. "Whoa. What kind of visit do you think this is?"

"I didn't mean…" My cheeks pulsed with heat. "I meant…Lifetime movies…kidnapping."

He laughed. "I'm joking. I knew what you meant. And, no. No kidnapping. Not tonight, anyway."

I moved out of the way to let Ryan in. He wasn't as tall as Chase, so he didn't fill the space the way Chase did when he'd been in my room. "So, what is it?" My eyes motioned to the bag.

Ryan held it out to me.

I took it from his hand. It was heavier than I expected. I leaned against my desk chair and looked inside. I laughed.

"So?" he asked.

I reached inside and pulled out a small billiards trophy. The golden plaque on the front of it read: *Billiards Champion Kappa Sigma Fraternity*. "Wow. I'm honored. Did you have this made?"

He nodded. "That's why it took a little while to come in."

"Well, thanks," I said, turning and placing it on my desk. "I think it looks perfect right there."

"And, for the sake of total disclosure, I may have had ulterior motives in bringing that by."

My eyebrows lifted in question.

"I was hoping I could maybe take you out," he said. "Seeing as though for some reason Chase already thinks I am."

I winced. "Yeah, about that."

"No need to explain," he said. "I played along, so he totally thinks we're hanging out tonight."

"Thanks."

He shrugged. "Just say you'll go out with me this weekend."

"Oh. I…"

His hopeful eyes stared into mine. I had no reason to turn him down, especially now that he covered for my little lie. Besides, I was single and could do what I pleased.

"Sure," I said.

A huge smile spread across his face. "Great. Let me get your phone."

I grabbed my phone off my desk, unlocked it, and handed it to him.

He dialed his number and his phone rang. He handed it back to me. "I'll call you this week."

I nodded. "Okay."

He moved to the door and pulled it open. "Bye Sophia," he said as he disappeared into the hallway.

I closed the door and moved to my bed. I dropped down with a *humph*, unsure how I felt about my impending plans with Ryan. Like I'd told Chantel after I met him at that first party, Ryan really wasn't my type. But he looked so hopeful when he asked, and I just couldn't bring myself to say no—or confess why I'd told Chase we were going out in the first place.

There was another knock on my door.

I stood and approached the door, thinking for sure Ryan must've left something behind and was coming back to retrieve it. I pulled open the door.

Chase stood there with his hands in his pockets and his eyes trained on mine. "Why was he in your room?"

"What?"

He brushed past me into the room. "Ryan. Why was he in here with you alone? I thought you were going out?"

I slammed the door and spun around, pissed at his tone and abrasiveness. "Don't even tell me this is somehow going to be about me being reckless again. Is it reckless to have a guy in my room?" I ticked my chin toward him. "Because *you're* in my room."

"You can trust me."

I scoffed. "Right. Trust is the first thing I think of when I think of you. Actually, right now, it's more like creepy stalker."

"I get it. I hurt your pride or something."

I sucked in a sharp breath. "My pride or something? Are you for real?"

"I'm just saying, you're mad at me. Fine. Whatever. But you need to listen to me."

"So, you're gonna dismiss my pride being hurt or whatever, but now I have to listen to you? *Seriously?*"

He dragged his hands through his hair. "God dammit, Soph. Stop putting yourself in bad situations."

"You know what?" I walked to the door. "I'm gonna take your advice." I yanked it open. "*You. You're* the bad situation. So, get out."

His teeth clenched and his jaw began to pulse.

"Thanks for worrying about my well-being," I said with an insincere smile. "But I'm good."

"That's not why I came by. We have our project."

A sarcastic laugh escaped me. "Not tonight we don't."

He stared at me long and hard, annoyance weighing heavy in his eyes like when we first met. He broke eye contact first and walked straight out the door without another word.

Good riddance, asshole.

CHAPTER FIFTEEN

I arrived early to Art History, taking my usual spot near the back. I checked my phone to be sure it was silenced then slipped it into my bag.

"Are you going out with him again?" Chase asked from the seat behind mine.

I didn't bother turning around. "That's not your seat."

"Are you gonna answer me?"

"Are you gonna leave me alone?" I countered. "Because first, you can't stand the sight of me, and now you've turned into some kind of creepy stalker."

"Answer the question."

"Yes."

"What?"

I huffed my frustration. "I just answered your question."

"So, you're going out with him again?"

I lifted my hands to my face and scrubbed them up down, needing to wake up from this craziness. "Please leave me alone."

"Chantel and I are going with you."

I spun around to glare at him. "Is something wrong with you? Like seriously messed up in your head?"

My question obviously confused him judging by the look on his face. "No."

"Are you sure? Because I think you're the crazy one I need to stay away from. You are seeing my roommate.

Which means you have no right to tell *me* what to do." I turned back around and despite his attempts to say more, I ignored him.

Going with him to the coast had been a bad decision. Nothing good came of it. He now thought he could tell me what to do and who to do it with. He clearly didn't get the memo. No one told me what to do. Not him. Not Chantel. I made my own decisions—good or bad, they were mine to make.

When the professor dismissed us, I took my time, hoping Chase would leave before me.

"We need to work on our project," he said, still seated in the seat behind mine.

I closed my eyes. Dealing with him was beginning to wear on me.

"Are you free tonight?"

I said nothing as I put my laptop into my backpack and stood up.

"Sophia?"

I swung my bag over my shoulders and secured it onto my back.

"I'll be in the media room at seven," he said, making no move to stand as I marched out of the lecture hall.

* * *

"Are you gonna meet him?" Valerie asked over dinner that night.

I shrugged. "I don't know. He's been acting so strange." I closed my eyes. "What am I saying? He only ever acts strange."

"He's always been a pretty chill guy," Valerie said.

"Are we talking about the same Chase?"

"Apparently, you just bring out the worst in him."

"Oh, yay me."

Valerie smiled before taking a bite of her salad. "You don't really have a choice, though, do you? He's your partner and your grade depends on both of you doing the work."

I released a deep breath, hating that she was right. I couldn't let my feelings about him affect my grade in the class. I could show up, watch the movies, and then write the paper without barely even having to talk to him.

Two hours later, I passed through the front door of the media room, scanning the dark room for Chase. He'd selected the same cubicle we sat in last time. I slipped into the empty seat beside him, and he jumped when he saw me.

"Hey," he said.

I removed my bag from my back and placed it on the floor.

"I already got the two movies," he said.

"Let me guess, the shortest ones?"

He shook his head. "Longest."

I heaved a deep breath, as two thoughts weighed on my mind. One, why did he want to spend time with me? And, two, what psychological issues did he suffer from? "I don't think I can make it through two movies tonight."

He shrugged. "I'm free tomorrow night if you are."

Ignoring his offer, I pulled our assignment sheet out of my bag, making sure I knew what the requirements were. It took no time for the woodsy scent of his cologne to drift toward me, working its way into my breaths. Why was it that hot guys always smelled good? Was it an unspoken requirement or something?

Chase switched on the old black and white movie, and I began taking notes. As the movie played, I sensed

Chase moving closer to me. Eventually, his arm rested against mine. *Oh, no you don't.* I shifted my arm away.

When he realized I was keeping my distance, his hand landed on my arm. I pulled my arm free of his grasp. "Cut it out."

"What?"

"You know what." I continued taking notes, and he stayed away from me for the remainder of the movie. When the credits rolled, I packed up without a word and walked out.

"Sophia," he called.

But I kept walking, knowing he had to return the movies to the counter and pack up. That gave me a head start. I hurried through the deserted floor toward the elevator, pressing the button and impatiently waiting for it to arrive.

I heard footsteps behind me and realized I'd failed to elude him.

"What are you doing?" Chase asked, his hands gripping the straps on his backpack.

"You know what I'm doing."

He released one of his straps and slipped his hand into mine.

My eyes shot down to where his big hand was linked with mine. I clenched my teeth. "Let go."

He shook his head as I tried releasing my hand.

"So, it's been you all along?" I said.

"What?"

"The one I need to be careful of."

He scoffed, before leading me away from the elevator.

"What the hell are you doing?" I asked, trying to resist him but he was too strong.

He said nothing.

My eyes shot around. There was no one around to help me if I screamed. I'd seen enough movies to know you never go to a second location with your kidnapper.

He moved us through the high shelves filled with old books until we were in a deserted corner of the library.

My heartbeat thrashed as he backed me into a wall, my backpack softening the hard wall behind me. His hands landed on the wall above me and he kept me still with the weight of his body.

"You are the most infuriating girl I've ever met," he said, his blue eyes staring into mine.

As nervous as I felt, I wouldn't let him see my fear. "Then let me go and you never have to see me again."

"Oh, I wish it were that simple."

I swallowed around the lump that had shot to my throat.

"I can't stop thinking about you, Soph."

My eyes widened.

"And it's driving me fucking crazy."

I said nothing, unable to peel my eyes away from his. How had he gone from kidnapping me to confessing his feelings for me?

"And the fact that Chantel showed up at my place Sunday night pissed me the hell off because I knew she'd make it known before I had a chance to explain to you."

"You have nothing to explain."

"I sent her away. I'm guessing she didn't tell you that."

I blinked, not knowing what to make of it. Who was lying? Chantel or Chase? "It doesn't matter. You and me, we're nothing to each other."

"Keep telling yourself that."

I opened my mouth to respond, but no words came out.

He shifted his hips so his very pronounced erection pressed against me. "I am perpetually hard whenever you're around. You invade my thoughts no matter what I'm doing. And, I keep trying to find reasons to be around you."

"You don't even like me," I countered.

He ignored my words. "Your smart mouth and witty comebacks keep me on my toes, and I can't wait to hear what's coming next."

"I don't even like *you*," I continued.

"And the fact that you're trying to ignore me and make me jealous with Ryan is eating away at me."

"What does that even mean?" I asked, at a complete loss over what was happening.

He lowered his hands and cupped my cheeks. They were warm and shockingly gentle. "That means I'm gonna kiss the fuck out of you right now."

My breath hitched as his mouth descended on mine. His tongue licked across my lips and, as much as I wanted to fight it, my body betrayed me and I let him in. My arms wrapped around his shoulders as my tongue tangled with his. I arched into him and I couldn't stop. This was a fight of wills. And neither of us was giving up. His hands drifted from my cheeks, down my sides, and around to my ass. Shamelessly, I rubbed against him. He groaned into my mouth. When we couldn't get close enough, he picked me up and my legs wrapped around his hips. He twisted us around and slammed my back into a shelf of books. The sound of books falling to the floor echoed around us. We laughed into each other's mouths, but neither of us pulled apart. My fingers tunneled into the back of his hair as I controlled the kiss—the best freaking kiss I'd ever had.

"The library is closing in five minutes," a librarian announced over the speaker system. "Please gather your belongings and exit now."

Chase pulled out of the kiss first, leaving my lips deliciously numb. His forehead dropped to mine as our chests heaved in tandem. "Holy. Shit."

His response elicited fluttering in my belly, but my brain warned me—like bellowing sirens going off in my head—to slow down. "Now that you got that out of your system, can I go?"

He lifted his head so he could see my face. "Are you serious? Because from where I'm standing with your ass in my hands and a hard-on for days, I'd say we're just getting started."

I closed my eyes, having no words for what he'd just said. It was all so freaking confusing. I hated him. And he hated me. So, why was the kiss so amazing? "It's gonna look a little strange to walk out like this," I said. "So, I think you need to put me down."

His low chuckle sent crazy vibrations through my nerve endings as he lowered me to my feet. "Come on." He grabbed hold of my hand and linked our fingers as we walked through the stacks toward the elevator. "Let me walk you home."

The word *home* created a giant cavern in my chest. I lived with *Chantel.* "I'll be fine."

He growled. "Why must you fight me?"

"Why must you act like my bodyguard?"

"Oh, I'd gladly guard your body," he said, stopping us at the elevator and kissing me again.

I released his hand and pushed him back. "Not here."

His brows dipped as I pressed the button for the elevator.

"I live with Chantel."

"I've been honest with her. She's the one who doesn't understand that we're not together."

"Well, this," I motioned between us, "Is not going any further until she knows in no uncertain terms that you two are not together nor will you ever be together."

"I've tried."

I cocked my head. "No, you've sent her mixed messages."

He inhaled deeply as the elevator arrived and we stepped inside. "It's complicated."

"Then explain it to me."

I watched the internal battle play out in his eyes. "I can't."

"Can't or won't?"

"I will tell you. I just need time."

"Take all the time you need. But until then…" I motioned between us again. "This can't happen."

His lips twisted regrettably as the elevator came to a stop and we walked out of the library. We stayed silent after that, both of us with our own thoughts.

Fifty yards or so away from my dorm, I stopped. "I can make it from here."

He nodded, understanding my concern. "Thanks for showing up tonight. I really didn't think you would."

"It was the right thing to do."

He nodded, and I could see he hoped our night would end a little more exciting. But he had a girl who thought she was his girlfriend. The same one who would not take the news that I was spending time with her "boyfriend" very well.

I turned away from him, but he grabbed my wrist, pulling me back into his chest. He ducked his head and captured my lips with his. My knees went weak beneath me, but I'd been serious. *This* couldn't happen like this.

I pulled back from the kiss, my chest heaving from the unexpected intrusion. I leveled Chase with my eyes, showing I was pissed by the reckless move, but he just smirked as he released my arm.

I twisted away from him, my eyes shooting around and making sure no one was around. I hurried toward the front door of the dorm without another word. I pulled out my ID to scan, but noise nearby caught my attention. It sounded like crying. I looked to the left, where the sound was coming from, and peered into the darkness.

A small silhouette of a girl with her knees tucked up and her arms wrapped around them on the grass against the building came into focus.

Please don't be Chantel. Please tell me she hadn't seen us.

I moved closer. "Valerie?"

Silence.

My feet carried me even closer. Valerie's features came into focus. "What's wrong?"

"Nothing," she said, her voice so small.

I stopped in front of her, noting the tears trailing down her cheeks. "What are you doing out here?"

She shrugged.

I pulled off my backpack and sat on the grass beside her. "You can talk to me. You know that, right?"

She nodded but said nothing.

"Did someone hurt you?"

She shrugged.

"Who?"

She shook her head.

"Come inside. You can come to my room."

She gasped. "I can't."

Anger clawed at my insides. "Did Chantel do something to you?"

She shrugged. "Valerie. You need to tell me. You are not her punching bag. I've seen the way she speaks to you. You don't deserve it."

"*Shhhhh*," she said, her eyes jumping around the darkness as if someone could hear us.

"You're scaring me. Please talk to me."

"I can't."

"Why not?"

She shook her head. "I said too much."

She said too much? She hadn't said anything.

She pushed herself to her feet.

I grabbed my backpack and jumped up, following her to the front door. "What does that mean?"

She scanned her card and we both walked inside. As we turned the corner for the stairs, Chantel stepped out in front us. Valerie and I both jumped.

"Oh my God," I said, nervous laughter tumbling out of me.

Chantel's eyes jumped between us. "What are you two doing?"

"Just taking a walk," I said.

Chantel eyed me. "With your backpack?"

"Oh, I…yup. With my backpack."

She glared at Valerie. "What's wrong with *you*?"

Valerie's eyes widened, and fear—true fear—flashed across her face. "Nothing."

"She slipped while we were walking," I lied. "Bumped her head."

"Clumsy me," Valerie added.

Chantel stared at us, unsure what to make of us standing there together. "Well, I'm heading to Chase's.

Don't wait up." She walked out of the building, and only then did we release our shaky breaths. Valerie for one reason and me for a completely different reason.

A tightness gripped my chest. Was she really going to Chase's? Had he called to ask her to come by so he could make it clear once again that they weren't together? Or had that all been a lie?

I walked Valerie to her room. Outside her door, she turned to me and threw her arms around me, hugging me tightly. "Thanks for knowing when to stop asking questions." She released me.

"I meant what I said. You can tell me anything."

She nodded, before punching in her code and disappearing inside her room.

I thought moving back to Texas would be easy. But nothing about being at Crestwood had been what I expected.

CHAPTER SIXTEEN

Chantel's bed was still made when I woke the next morning. A jealous pit formed in my stomach. Did I have the right to be jealous? Maybe Chase just needed to console her. Or maybe she ended up in one of her sisters' rooms, needing her friends to console her. I was sure he'd have an explanation when I arrived to History through Film. The problem with that? He never made it to class.

"Sophia?"

I'd just stepped out of the building when I twisted toward the sound of my name.

Ryan moved toward me with a big smile on his face. "Hey."

My shoulders slumped, hoping the voice belonged to someone else. "Hey."

"So, I was thinking about this weekend."

"Can you walk with me and tell me?" I asked as I continued toward my next class.

"Sure. I was talking to Chantel and Chase last night," he said.

My stomach dropped. They'd *all* been talking the previous night?

"And they want all four of us to go out," he explained.

They wanted us to go on a double date? There was still a *they*?

What universe was I living in? Was this some kind of joke? Was this Chantel's way of staking her claim? Was this Chase's way of showing me he'd never be done with Chantel? Or, was he just trying to have his cake and eat it too? My hopeful side wanted to believe he just needed to keep his eyes on Ryan and me. But if that were the case, why was he taking Chantel? *FML.*

"And you really want to go with them?" I asked Ryan.

He shrugged. "Sounds like it'll be fun."

"And if I say it sounds terrible?"

"I'll tell you what. Let's give it a try. If it sucks, we'll bail."

I sobered my features, trying not to either scream or cry because right then, my emotions were so all over the place I didn't know which way was up and which way was down. But I did know Ryan wanted to take me out. And, he'd been nice to me from the very beginning with no strings attached. I didn't want my problems to affect him. "Sure. Whatever."

"Great." His face lit up. "I'll pick you up at seven on Friday. Does that work?"

I stopped in front of my building. "Yup."

He smiled. "See you then."

I turned away from him, wondering if he understood how messed up this whole thing was. Because if it turned out that he did, and he was in on it, this place and these people were even more screwed up than I imagined.

* * *

I thought about not going to the media room that night. Everything in me told me it was a terrible idea. But I said I'd be there, and whether or not Chase had shown up to class or not, the plan was to meet there.

So, after thirty minutes of sitting in the media room waiting for Chase, I watched the movie alone. I took notes and then left, walking home in the darkness all by myself. And the crazy thing was…I made it home unscathed.

My heart? Not so much.

CHAPTER SEVENTEEN

Chase wasn't in Art History on Thursday or History through Film on Friday. Regardless of his absence, I wrote the paper and submitted it through the portal. Everything in me told me not to put his name on it. But in the end, against my better judgment, I added it.

When I returned to the dorm later, Chantel wasn't in our room. With all her pledge events, I barely saw her. But I hoped her absence meant she decided to bail on our double date. It was bound to be a shit show, and she had to know that.

Regardless of where Chantel was, I showered and got ready. Because there was one thing I was sure of. I planned to look good.

I blew dry my hair and curled it in loose waves. I slipped on tight leather pants I saved for special occasions and a sleeveless, low cut, leopard print shirt. I hooked a silver necklace around my neck that hung between my breasts and disappeared into my cleavage. Then, I put on makeup, opting for smoky eyes, and adding a black eyeliner wing to give my eyes a dramatic and mysterious look. I added some blush and topped off the look with red lipstick.

I stared at myself in the mirror, admiring my work. I didn't enjoy dressing up. But tonight, looking good was imperative. There was a knock on the door. I checked the time. Ryan was ten minutes early.

I pulled open the door, laughing when I found Valerie standing there with her mouth hanging open. "You look hot."

"Hold on. I haven't even put on my heels yet."

"Ryan is going to die," she said, stepping inside and closing the door. "So is Chase."

Hopefully.

I reached into my closet and pulled out black, peep toe, low-rise boots and slipped them on.

Valerie gawked at me like she'd never seen me before. "Holy hell, girl. Why don't you dress like that more often?"

I chuckled, happy my friend was back to normal. The crying version made me nervous since she was usually so upbeat around me. "Cut it out. It's a little makeup."

"And a whole lot of hotness."

There was another knock on the door. I walked over and opened it. Ryan stood there in jeans and a dark gray shirt. His mouth hung open. "Holy shit."

Valerie walked over. "Doesn't she look gorgeous?"

With wide eyes, Ryan nodded.

"I'm ready," I said to him.

We all walked out together, Valerie heading to her dorm room.

"Bye, Val," I yelled after her.

She waved. "Don't have too much fun, you crazy kids!"

I laughed.

"You look beautiful, Sophia," Ryan said as we made our way downstairs.

"Thanks. Where are we going?"

"We're meeting Chase and Chantel for dinner."

"You sure they're still showing up? Chantel wasn't at the dorm."

"Yeah, she got ready at the frat."

The knot in my stomach grew. "Great."

Our conversation as we drove to dinner flowed easily. But our conversations always flowed easily. That wasn't the problem. I just didn't feel it with Ryan.

When we arrived at the restaurant, Ryan asked me to wait, getting out of the car and coming to my side to open my door. My heart began to race as he helped me out, and we moved closer to the entrance. Once we stepped inside, I realized we were in a noisy pub. *Thank God.* I wouldn't have been able to take a sit-down meal in a quiet restaurant. The pounding of my heart alone would have been filling the uncomfortable silence.

The hostess pointed us toward a high-top table where Chantel and Chase were already sitting. I pulled in a deep breath. They didn't notice us at first. But I could tell the second Chase did because his eyes widened. Chantel glanced over to see what caught Chase's attention. Her bitch stare fell firmly into place.

"Hi guys," I said, sliding onto the stool beside Chantel as if we were besties.

"Hey," Chase said as Ryan slipped onto the stool beside him.

"Hi," Chantel said, a tightness to her lips as her eyes moved over me. "I didn't realize virgins dressed like that."

I inhaled sharply, trying to stop the embarrassment flooding my body.

"*Chantel*," Chase chastised.

Ryan tensed beside me.

Sorry, dude. You weren't getting any action tonight. And, yes. This is why I told you this was a terrible idea.

"Yup," I said, trying my damnedest to save face. "We virgins do a lot of things. We ride in cars with boys. We may even let them kiss us good night if it's before curfew, of course."

Ryan snickered beside me. Chase stifled a grin.

Chantel sipped her drink, trying to maintain the upper hand she thought she had after outing me.

"But you know something we don't do," I continued, feeling bold. "We don't snoop through other people's personal things." She may have started this battle of wits, but I was going to finish it.

"You just crush on other girl's men," she clipped.

My eyes cut to Chase. His averted mine. *Chicken.*

"We may even do that," I agreed.

The waitress approached and asked if Ryan and I needed a drink. "Tequila shots," I said, thankful for the intrusion.

Ryan laughed beside me. "Looks like it's gonna be that kind of night."

I stared across the table at Chase. "Yeah. The reckless kind."

Luckily, talk of my virginity ceased and the Tequila shots arrived. We all held them up in the center of the table. "To new friends," I said.

"To new friends," Ryan said, tapping my shot glass.

We threw back our shots. Chase and Chantel threw back theirs without even toasting.

I winced as the sting of Tequila burned all the way down my throat.

The waitress returned once our empty shot glasses were down on the table. "Another round?"

"Yes," I answered for everyone.

"Hey, Sophia," Chase said. "Are you even old enough to drink?"

"Of course, I am," I said, shooting daggers across the table at him.

The waitress looked to me and Ryan. "Oh, did I forget to check your IDs?"

Ryan slipped his ID out of his pocket and handed it to her. I didn't have my fake ID with me, and I couldn't hand over my license that said I was nineteen—for another two weeks.

She handed him back his ID and looked to me.

"I forgot mine at home," I said.

"Sorry, honey. No ID, no drinks."

Chantel laughed beside me.

I glared at Chase, wondering why he'd embarrass me like that. Maybe he and Chantel had more in common than I thought. Maybe they did belong together.

We ordered dinner and the conversation between Ryan and Chase jumped from football to their frat to a rumor about a professor and his student. Chantel and I barely spoke. I wondered why Chase was so worried about me being alone with Ryan if they were such good friends.

Thankfully, dinner came and I didn't need to speak. After finishing off my pasta, I excused myself for the restroom. Once inside, I stared in the mirror. I almost didn't recognize myself. Why had I tried so hard to make Chase jealous? Why did I care when he was clearly playing games? I freshened up, then reluctantly returned to the table.

"We're gonna head to the beach," Ryan informed me.

"Whose idea was that?" I asked.

"Mine," Chase said. "I just love a nice drive to the coast."

It took everything in me not to say I didn't feel well, but I knew what Chase was doing. And if I bailed now, he won. "Great. I love the coast. Skinny dipping is actually on my bucket list." I looked at Ryan. "I think you might be the only one here who doesn't know I have a jar full of bucket list wishes." I glanced around the table. "Anyone up for skinny dipping?"

I watched Chase's tough exterior falter under my words. Served him right for suggesting a drive to the coast.

"I'm in," Ryan said.

"Chantel?" I challenged.

"If Chase does," she said.

He stared across the table at me. "We'll see."

CHAPTER EIGHTEEN

We piled into Chase's black SUV. Chantel took the front, and Ryan and I climbed into the back. I stared out my window as we drove wondering whose convertible we'd taken to the coast *and* what the hell I'd gotten myself into. I had no desire to skinny dip with any of them. I just needed them to know they couldn't make me look like a fool.

"So, Sophia. When was the last time you've been to the coast?" Chase asked.

And the hits just keep on coming. "Oh, funny story." I met his eyes in the rearview mirror. "Some guy thought he could get with me by taking me to the coast. He picked me up in a convertible and everything."

"I'm glad it didn't work out. Since I'm with you tonight and not that guy," Ryan said with a smirk.

"Yeah. It was a total letdown," I said, holding Chase's eyes in the rearview mirror.

"How's your pledge class, Chantel?" Ryan asked.

She twisted in her seat. "Great. Most of them are legacies from wealthy families which is really amazing. How about you guys? Chase hasn't said much about your new pledge class."

Ryan shrugged. "Well, they do a nice job cleaning up our shit after parties."

"That's how you judge a good pledge class?" I asked.

"Pretty much," he said.

I shook my head, amused.

We reached the beach in record time. Chase parked in the empty parking lot, pulling up to the dune separating the parking lot from the beach.

"Do you have any towels?" Chantel asked him.

"I may have a couple in the back." He opened his door, and we were treated to a gust of salty air and the sound of crashing waves nearby. Chase circled to the back to check for towels, grabbing a couple as the rest of us stepped out of the car.

The gusty beach air was such a contrast to the inland air, but I breathed it in, reveling in the scent and feel and wishing it didn't remind me of my day with Chase. I walked over to him and pulled one of the towels from his hand.

He looked like he wanted to say something, but he didn't.

Chantel grabbed another towel from him.

We made our way onto the sand. I stopped, slipping off my shoes before following the group down to the water's edge. The guys slipped off their shoes and socks, while Chantel kicked off hers.

My heartbeat kicked up a notch, and I wondered if the rest of them would be stripping down. "You guys still going in?"

Ryan pulled his shirt over his head. With the moon almost full, the beach wasn't completely blanketed in darkness, so I could see the cross tattoo across his back. *It was always the quiet ones.* He slipped off his jeans and stood in front of us in only his boxers. "Give me the towel, Sophia," he said to me. "I'll hold it up while you get undressed."

I glanced to Chase who looked ready to hurt someone. "Okay."

Ryan held the towel up around me as I shimmied out of my leather pants. Those would be a bitch to get back on while wet. I pulled off my top, leaving me in my black panties and bra, and wrapped the towel around me. I eyed Chantel and Chase. "You two gonna wimp out?"

Chase pulled off his charcoal Henley. *Holy shit.* The ridges defining his muscles and six-pack abs left a lot to be desired. I tried not to stare for fear of Chantel rearing her claws, but my *God.* A vision of his chest pressed against mine in the library flooded my brain. And all those emotions rushed back as he dropped his jeans and stood in front of us in his black boxer briefs. I'd felt what lay hidden inside his briefs against me in the library, but now I could see the outline, and my thighs quivered.

This was bad. This was *very* bad.

"Fine," Chantel sighed.

Chase moved toward her to hold up the towel so she could get undressed, but she shooed him away. "I'm no virgin. Let 'em look." She shimmied out of her short denim skirt and pulled her shirt over her head, leaving her in a thong and bra. The girl had a perfect body. No wonder she didn't mind flaunting it.

Ryan took off for the water, running in and howling with laughter. Under the water, he removed his boxers and tossed them onto the beach. I laughed as I grabbed them and moved them away from the shoreline.

I dropped my towel and jogged in next, screaming when the cold water hit my skin, stealing my breath away. I could see Chase and Chantel standing on the beach watching, so I lowered myself in the water up to my neck. *Might as well check this one off my list.* I unfastened my bra and shimmied out of my panties. I balled them up and tossed them onto the sand.

"Nice," Ryan said, keeping an appropriate distance, given I was naked under the water.

Chase dropped his briefs right on the beach and walked toward the water.

I couldn't take my eyes off his dark figure moving into the water. I wasn't sure if it was the temperature of the water making me tremble or the sight of Chase naked.

"Jesus Christ! It's cold," he cried out.

Ryan and I laughed, understanding his shock.

"Come on, Chantel," Ryan called to her, standing alone on the beach.

My gaze wandered toward Chase who stared back at me.

Ryan splashed water at me, pulling my attention from Chase.

Startled, by the unexpected blast of bitterly cold water stinging my face, I swept an armful of water his way. "Not nice!"

He laughed. "Just making your bucket list adventure one to remember."

"Oh, it's memorable all right." I glanced to Chase who now stared out at the ocean.

"This is stupid and I'm cold," Chantel said. "I'm going back to the car."

I rolled my eyes at Ryan.

"It *is* friggin' cold," Chase agreed. "You guys almost ready?"

Ryan looked to me.

I nodded, my teeth now chattering.

"I'll grab your stuff and turn away so you have privacy," Ryan said.

I watched as he and Chase made their way out of the water, stifling a smile at their bare white asses. I couldn't hear them over the crashing of the waves, but their heads whipped from side to side as they walked all over the area of beach where we'd come in from.

"What's wrong?" I called.

Ryan glanced over his shoulder at me, careful not to reveal his naked man parts. "We can't find our stuff."

"Did we drift?" I asked.

Chase shook his head. "Chantel must've taken everything."

"You've got to be kidding me. Even the towels?" I called.

He nodded.

"Well, you head to the car," I said to Chase. "Ryan can block me."

Several emotions flash across Chase's face. Even in the darkness, I could see he didn't like that idea.

Sorry, dude. A double date was your idea.

Chase turned and retreated to the car.

Once he disappeared on the other side of the dune, Ryan turned away from me and I hurried out, cursing the cold air that bit away at my skin. I grabbed hold of his shoulders and walked directly behind him.

"She's such a bitch," he said as we hurried toward the car.

"Why is that?"

"Because she can be."

"That's a terrible answer."

He laughed. "No, seriously. People don't ever speak up when it comes to her. They allow her to be awful. You don't and she hates that. *And,*" he continued. "She sees the way Chase looks at you and it drives her crazy."

"How does he look at me?"

"Like you're his."

I said nothing, though his words brought a tiny sliver of warmth to my frigid body.

We finally reached the car. Chantel sat in the front seat, avoiding all of our pissed faces. Chase stood outside with a towel outstretched and his eyes looking elsewhere. Ryan grabbed the towel and wrapped it around me, making sure not to touch or look at any part of me.

"Thank you," I said. "Let me just put my clothes on and then you can have the towel."

"Ummmm…" Chase began, still averting his gaze.

Sudden dread swept over me. "What?"

"Your clothes are soaking wet."

"Of course they are," I said, knowing Chantel had purposely done something to them while we were in the water.

"Dude, rein your girl in," Ryan said, anger coloring his tone. "She's always such a God damned bitch."

Chase shook his head, looking just as pissed as Ryan and I were.

It was a quiet ride back to the restaurant to get Ryan's car. I didn't want to give Chantel the satisfaction of a reaction, so I said nothing, sitting in the back seat with the towel wrapped around me tightly. I caught Chase's eyes in the rearview mirror throughout the ride but avoided looking back at him.

We finally pulled into the parking lot at the restaurant.

"I'll bring Sophia back to the dorm," Chase said. "She already got my seat wet. No need to get yours wet."

Ryan looked to me in question.

"I'm fine," I assured Ryan. Besides, I didn't want to get out of the car to get into another one while wearing only a towel, and the campus was only five minutes away. "Thanks for…an interesting night."

Ryan smiled, lowering his voice. "Next time just you and me."

My lips curved, not confirming or rejecting his offer.

He stepped out of the car. "Later, guys."

Once he closed the door, the car was eerily silent.

Chase pulled out of the parking lot, turning up the music so no conversation could take place. The five-minute ride felt like an hour, but he finally pulled to a stop in front of our dorm. I opened my door and stepped out, not looking back or saying a word to either of them. I slammed the door and made my way inside.

Once upstairs in my room, I grabbed my shower caddy and took a nice long hot shower, washing off the saltwater as well as the disgust I'd felt toward both Chantel and Chase. I'd been embarrassed, humiliated, and made to look like a fool—yet again by both of them.

I returned to the room in my sleep shorts and top, stopping in the doorway when I found Chantel alone in our room crying on her bed. I said nothing, just closed the door behind me and put my shower caddy in the closet. I made my way over to my bed and slipped under the covers, not about to console her after how totally bitchy she'd been.

Silence filled the room for a long stretch, her soft sniffles piercing the quiet every now and then.

"I know I'm a bitch," she finally said.

There was nothing to say. She was.

"I wanted to embarrass you tonight."

I stayed silent.

"But in the end, it didn't matter. Chase wants nothing to do with me."

My stomach dipped, but I gave myself a much-needed internal tsk. *He was just on a date with someone else! He just embarrassed you at the restaurant! He was playing with your feelings, and that is not all right!*

"Don't act like you're not thrilled," Chantel said.

I said nothing. I had nothing to do with their relationship.

"We could've been friends, me and you. But you're always off with Valerie. You turn your nose up at me and my sorority."

I finally spoke. "Valerie and I are similar."

She scoffed. "You don't know the real Valerie."

I liked to think I did, but I kept that to myself.

"Chase wants you, you know?"

I said nothing.

"Don't think I don't know about your secret meet-ups at the library. I have eyes everywhere."

"We're partners in history class," I explained.

"Didn't think to mention that before now?"

She had a point. I hadn't mentioned it.

"Yeah, your paper wouldn't have disappeared had you thought to."

I felt the blood drain from my face as I finally turned to look at her. "What?"

"Oh," she said all sweet. "I just meant I would've been able to help you with that tricky portal."

Son of a bitch.

She stood from her bed and walked to the closet, grabbing some clothes and stuffing them into an overnight bag. "Andi's roommate moved back home. I'm gonna stay with her for the rest of the weekend." She moved to the door and grabbed hold of the handle. "I just need…space."

Glad she was leaving, I said nothing. I needed space from her too.

"But, Sophia?" She pulled open the door. "If you think you're gonna get with him now, you need to watch yourself." She switched off the light. "Payback's a bitch."

She turned and walked out, letting the door slam behind her and shrouding the room in complete darkness.

CHAPTER NINETEEN

"So, what'd you do?" Valerie asked over breakfast Saturday morning.

My eyes shot around, making sure no one in the dining hall could hear me. Chantel did, in fact, have eyes everywhere. "Drove home in a towel."

Valerie shook her head. "She's so twisted."

"She said if I go out with Chase, I better watch myself."

Her voice became serious. "She's not kidding."

"Why are you so scared of her?" I asked.

Valerie's eyes drifted from mine, as if she was considering answering me but unsure if she should.

Before Valerie could say anything, Tina passed by our table. She didn't stop, but gave a little wave and said, "Hey, Val."

"Hey," Valerie said back to her as she walked away.

"Did she forget my name?" I asked.

"She's just like Chantel. Hot and cold."

"You sure Chantel didn't already spread the word to ice me out now that Chase cut her loose?"

"There's that too," Valerie said. "But you don't seem like someone who's fazed by her threats."

"I'm not."

"Are you gonna see Ryan again?"

I shook my head. "He texted last night about going out again."

"And?"

"I let him down easy."

"Poor guy."

"I'm sure he'll bounce back. Kappa Sigmas seem to have their pick of willing females."

Her mouth opened. "Do you know what would be awesome?"

I shook my head.

"Chantel has a pledge event next weekend. Since we don't have a house, she's taking the pledges to a hotel for some bonding activities."

"Sounds awful."

"Oh, it will be. Luckily, I'm not invited. The only sisters she's taking are Tina and Andi."

"Lucky you. So, what would be awesome?"

Her eyes lit up. "The Kappa Sigmas are having a huge party on Saturday. Word will definitely get back to her if we show up there and there's not a damn thing she can do about it while she's with the pledges."

I laughed. "I didn't think you had it in you."

She laughed. "Oh, I have it in me."

* * *

I walked into History through Film Monday morning, keeping my eyes on my seat and not on Chase who was already there. I slipped into my chair and pulled out my laptop.

"So," he said, turning his body to face me. "When are you gonna let me take you out on a real date?"

My eyes cut to his. "Oh, I'm sorry. Did you say something? My underage ears didn't quite hear you."

He sat back and crossed his arms, a soft chuckle leaving his lips.

Professor Irons began his lecture.

I focused on him, trying to ignore Chase's eyes boring into the side of my head for the remainder of the class.

When the professor dismissed us, I tried to get out of there as quickly as I could, but Chase caught up with me outside the building. "You trying to avoid me?"

"Yup." I shot him a sideways glance as I kept walking toward my next class. "Friday sucked."

"It was the only way I could keep an eye on you," he said, keeping pace with my strides.

"You're really starting to scare me," I said.

"I'm not the one you need to be scared of," he said.

"Yeah. Chantel's pretty scary."

A flicker of amusement lit his eyes.

"She says she has eyes everywhere," I said. "I'd be worried about being seen with me if I were you."

"I told you. I'm not scared of her." His eyes grew serious. "I'm sorry it took me so long to end things."

"You claim the two of you were never together, so…" I shrugged.

We arrived at the building where I had my next class. Chase stopped and I kept walking. "See ya," I called as I climbed the steps, not bothering to look back.

I wouldn't lie. Chase asking me out created that warm fuzzy feeling inside me that usually came whenever he was near. But, if he thought for one second that I'd drop everything because now he'd finally broken things off with Chantel, he didn't know me very well.

* * *

On Tuesday, I arrived to Art History right on time, inwardly groaning when I spotted Chase in the seat behind mine again. The lecture hall had five hundred seats. Why did he need to sit behind me? I slipped into my seat without looking at him.

"Go out with me this weekend," he said from behind me.

The professor began speaking, so I ignored him. Halfway through her lecture on Picasso, the girl next to me handed me a folded-up sheet of paper. I stared down at the paper then looked to her in question.

Her eyes flicked over her shoulder.

Of course.

I took the paper from her and covertly unfolded it in my lap so Chase couldn't see over my shoulder.

Put me out of my misery and go out with me this weekend.

I fought the urge to smile, tucking the note in my bag and continuing to listen to the lecture.

He was going to have to work harder than that.

* * *

I arrived to History through Film right on time on Wednesday. Chase, again, was already there, playing on his phone. He didn't glance up when I slipped into my chair.

"Good morning, ladies and gentlemen," Professor Irons said. "Today we're going to discuss the difference between the bombing of Pearl Harbor as depicted in 2001's *Pearl Harbor* and 1970's *Tora! Tora! Tora!*"

My phone buzzed in my back pocket. As soon as Professor Iron's turned to cue up the first film, I slipped my phone into my lap and peeked at the screen. **I can't be held responsible for my actions when he shuts off these lights.**

I sobered my features and responded to Chase's text. **Would you like me to leave then?**

The raspy sound of his chuckle carried my way, but I focused on the front of the classroom where Professor Irons had started the movie right at the bombing scene.

Intense echoes of explosions and gunfire on-screen reverberated off the walls of the small classroom.

My phone buzzed again in my lap.

I fought the urge to look, keeping my eyes on the film. I knew Chase was watching, and it made it even harder to resist looking.

As Professor Irons stopped the first film and called up the next, my phone buzzed again in my lap, reminding me of my unread text.

I finally peeked at my screen.

I'm sorry things between us haven't been easy.

Another text popped on my screen. **I plan to change that.**

I closed my eyes, praying for the strength to walk out of that class when we were dismissed and keep Chase Reed at arm's length. At least until I knew for sure if he was even someone I wanted to invest time in.

He was right. Nothing about us had been easy.

My phone buzzed again.

I never should have allowed her to speak to you the way she did.

I could feel my strength wavering. I responded to his text the only way I could. **Yup. You suck.**

I didn't peek over to see his reaction. And, he left me alone for the remainder of the class.

When Professor Irons dismissed us, I stood. I expected Chase to do or say something. He didn't. I walked out into the hallway and toward the stairwell. Once I stepped outside, I realized Chase hadn't followed me, and I wasn't sure how I felt about that. Was he giving up that easily?

On Thursday, Chase was back in his regular seat at the other side of the lecture hall. He didn't pass me another note; he didn't even acknowledge that I was there. Was he trying a new approach, or did he not like having to work so hard?

On Friday, he walked into History through Film two minutes late, not even glancing to me when he sat. His silence continued throughout the whole fifty-minute lecture. At the end of class, Professor Irons explained that our next film project would be due in two weeks, then dismissed us.

I gathered my belongings.

"So, when do you want to get started?" Chase asked me.

I glanced to him. "Oh, you're speaking to me again?"

He cocked his head.

"Well, you know where to find me when you're ready to begin the project."

"See? You say that. But if I show up at your room, how do I know you'll even answer?"

I shrugged. "I guess you'll just need to show up." I spun away from him and walked out of class, wondering if he'd actually show up.

* * *

"Chase showed," Valerie announced as she entered her room.

I winced as I looked up from her bed where I'd been doing my homework while trying to avoid Chase. "Was he pissed I wasn't there?"

Her nose wrinkled. "I don't know. He threw back his head and laughed when I told him you went out."

I studied her face. "He laughed?"

"Yeah. Like he almost expected it." She dropped down onto her bed beside me. "I think you put him through enough this week, don't you? I think it's about time you figure out what's going on between the two of you. You both owe it to yourselves."

My lips twisted as I contemplated her question. "Soon."

CHAPTER TWENTY

Valerie and I got out of the Uber and walked into Kappa Sigma Saturday night. I left the leopard print at home, opting for torn jeans and a green shirt. People filled the front porch and all the rooms as we made our way toward the basement. I kept my eyes out for Chase, but I didn't see him. Downstairs, the music roared, drinks were flowing, and people all around us were dancing.

"Let's get a beer," Valerie said, weaving us through the crowd.

The guy behind the bar, likely one of the new pledges, poured two cups from the keg and handed them to us. We made our way to the dance floor, laughing and moving to the music for a while. A short time later, I noticed Valerie's eyes latch on to something over my shoulder. I twisted around and there he was, standing on the stairs, towering over everyone and searching the room. Our eyes collided.

My heart fluttered as I held his gaze, now staring across the crowded space at only me. He didn't move to come down. He just stared, and the corners of his lips twitched. *What are you gonna do now, frat boy?*

I turned back to Valerie and continued dancing with her, throwing my arms in the air and moving my hips to the music.

Time seemed to stall as two strong hands grasped my hips and a hard chest pressed to my back.

Valerie's eyes widened as she stifled a grin.

Lips moved beside my ear. "I guess you'll just need to show up, huh?" Chase's voice sent goosebumps dancing across my skin. *Damn him.*

"Oops. Was I not there?"

"No, you weren't."

"Well, I'm here now."

"Yeah." He dragged his chin alongside my neck and more goosebumps erupted. "And that makes me very happy."

I continued moving to the music with his hands on my hips, but I said nothing.

"Have I mentioned that you naked underwater last weekend did some uncontrollable things to my body."

I clenched my thighs as heat shot to my core.

Valerie winked. "I'm gonna get another beer." She turned away from us and disappeared amongst the moving bodies.

I spun around and slipped my arms around Chase's neck.

His hands shifted to my back as his eyes gazed into mine, like no one else occupied that crowded basement. "Hi."

"Hi."

"Am I forgiven?"

In that moment, with the music pumping through the room, his arms around me, and his hopeful eyes anticipating my response, I could only nod.

The smile that swept across his face did crazy things to *my* body. He leaned in, his lips dangerously close to mine.

"Remember," I warned. "Chantel has eyes everywhere."

"Then let 'em watch." His lips crashed into mine, his tongue sweeping inside my mouth. I tried pulling back but he wouldn't have it; he kept our mouths locked as his tongue tangled with mine in a room full of people. Silence drowned out the noise around us, and all I could focus on was his strong hands holding my ass to him, his erection pressing into me, and his mouth devouring mine. This wasn't the frantic kiss in the library. This was intimate. This was binding. This was everything I wanted in that moment—even in a room full of people.

We eventually split apart, our chests heaving as we drank each other in with our eyes, both of us wanting more.

"Let's go back to your room," he said.

My brows shot up.

"I want to spend time with you, Soph." He motioned around us. "Without all of this."

I considered his request. But I'd come with Valerie and I didn't want to leave her alone.

"She's fine," he said, reading my mind and pointing her out with a group of girls drinking at the bar.

"Let me just go tell her."

He grabbed hold of my hand and walked with me. When Valerie spotted us, she didn't even wait for me to say anything; she shooed us away. "Go. Get outta here."

I smiled and mouthed, "Thank you."

"Have fun," she called as we headed to the stairs.

"I just gotta grab something upstairs," Chase said as we hit the main floor.

"I'll wait."

"Nope." He pulled me up the stairs with him and led me down the second-floor hallway. There were people partying in their rooms. Chase stopped at his closed door and pulled out his key. I looked across the hall and saw

Ryan in a room with a group of guys. A smattering of liquor bottles and prescription bottles filled his dresser. Ryan looked up and we made eye contact, then he gestured to someone to close the door.

"You did this on purpose," I said to Chase as Ryan's door slammed.

"What?" Chase asked as he unlocked his door and pushed it open.

"You brought me up here so Ryan could see us together."

A smile spread across his face as he led me into his room.

"That was mean."

He closed the door behind us. "I did you a favor. Now you don't have to have the awkward it's-not-you-it's-me talk."

"I already had that talk."

His brows shot up. "Yeah?"

"Yeah. So, next time you're thinking about doing something crappy, don't. Ryan's always been nice to me. And, I'm not someone to rub something in someone else's face."

"Sorry," he said, and I hoped he understood where I was coming from.

I looked around his room as he grabbed some clothes from his drawer and stuffed them into his backpack. His bed was neatly made, no clothes lay anywhere in the room, and he had one picture on his nightstand. I picked it up, hoping it wasn't a photo of him and Chantel. Relief washed over me when I found it was a picture of him standing between an older man and woman. "Are these your parents?"

He glanced to the picture and nodded.

"No siblings?"

He shook his head. "Nope. Just me."

"Were you that much of a handful?"

A slow smile spread across his lips. "Depends who you ask. My mom would say I can do no wrong."

"She clearly doesn't know you."

He laughed.

I examined the photo. "You look like your mom."

"I'll be sure to tell her you said that. Everyone says I look like my dad."

He and his dad had the same icy blue eyes. But the rest of his features, including those faint dimples, belonged to his mom. "It's a nice picture."

"Yeah? I'm gonna have to replace it with a picture of you and me."

I rolled my eyes. "If whatever this is even lasts past the weekend."

"Come again?" he said, more of a threat than a question.

"Well, you do tend to piss me off whenever you open your mouth."

"Oh, I don't plan on doing a whole lot of talking tonight," he said with a smirk on his lips.

I swallowed down my sudden nerves. I hadn't held onto my virginity this long to give it up to a guy who just kind of broke up with my roommate who wasn't really his girlfriend. I thought we'd get to know each other before sex was even on the table.

Was I naïve to have thought that?

"Stop stressing, Soph. I *know*. And I'm not about to force myself on you tonight. I was joking."

I released a silent breath.

He threw his backpack onto his back and reached for my hand again. As we made our way downstairs and out the front door, I prayed I wasn't making a huge mistake.

CHAPTER TWENTY-ONE

I expected Chase to walk to the parking lot behind the frat house to grab his SUV, but he led me down the front sidewalk. "You don't mind walking, do you?"

I shook my head as we headed toward my dorm, the music from the frat house fading into the darkness. Crickets chirped and the light of the partial moon accompanied us as we walked in comfortable silence, alone and free to do as we pleased.

"If you didn't show up at the party," Chase said, "I was gonna show up at your dorm."

"You could've just sent an Uber," I deadpanned.

Laughter burst out of him, and the sweet sound brought on my own laughter.

He squeezed my hand. "I'm glad you came." He tugged me in a different direction than my dorm. "I wanna show you something." He led me toward the quad. The area was deserted and peaceful late at night—such a contrast to a busy school day when students crisscrossed in every different direction.

Chase moved us toward one of the old cobblestone buildings surrounding the quad. An old plaque on the front of the building read: *Established in 1885*. We walked around to the side of the two-story building. An old metal ladder ran from the top of the building to just even with the first-floor window. "Here." Chase stepped behind me, grasping my hips. "Reach up and climb to the top."

I looked back at him, confused. "What?"

"Just reach up and I'm gonna lift you."

"Ummm…"

"Oh, damn. Can you not climb with your knee?"

"My knee's fine. But, are you coming, too?"

He laughed. "No, I'm gonna leave you up there all alone."

I reached for the first bar on the ladder as Chase lifted me off my feet. I grasped hold of it and pulled myself up to the second rung, climbing the rest of the way like a girl not used to climbing ladders. When I finally reached the top, I threw my leg over the turret-type ledge less gracefully than I wished and climbed to the flat surface of the roof. Though only two stories high, my legs shook beneath me as I looked down at the pavement below.

The thought of Sydney Lane jumping from *four* flights was astounding—not to mention heartbreaking.

I watched Chase stealthily climb the ladder, making it look so easy. He soon stood beside me. The darkness concealed us on top of the roof as we took in the view. The campus from that vantage point took my breath away. The old buildings were all dimly lit by a small light out front. The security lights in the corners of the quad cast a dim blue light on the sidewalk beneath them. The magnolia trees, though cloaked by night, created their very own wall of shadows all about.

Chase moved behind me, his chest pressing to my back as his arms slipped around me. He locked his hands on my stomach and rested his chin on my shoulder. "Isn't it beautiful from up here?"

I nodded. "Is this your spot?"

"My spot?"

"Yeah, where you take all the girls?"

He chuckled, the vibration moving against my back. "Every last one of them."

"No, seriously? How'd you know about it?"

"The Kappa Sigmas bring their pledges up here."

"For what?"

"If I told you, I'd be breaking a century-old frat secret."

"You're joking."

He chuckled. "I'm not. But I will tell you. They make pledges stand on the ledge of the roof and repeat the frat's motto."

"*Wow*. Such a *big* secret," I teased.

"Naked," he added.

I snorted. "Did you have to do that at your old fraternity?"

"I'll deny it if anyone asks."

"So, that's a yes?"

He shrugged. "I've done a lot of things I'm not proud of."

I wondered if that was his way of apologizing for all the things he'd done to hurt me.

He lifted his hands to my arms, moving them up and down my skin. "Jesus. You're shaking." He slipped his hand into mine. "Come on. I just wanted to show you the best view on campus. But it's getting cold."

"Thanks for taking me up here. It really is a beautiful view."

"We can come back when it's warmer," he said.

I nodded, liking the idea that he was planning a future event for us. Like it was his way of saying this wasn't only about tonight.

"It's even better at sunset."

"So, you do come up here a lot."

"Yeah, I come up here a lot. But *alone*. When I need a break from the frat."

Something about the way he stressed alone provided me with more reassurances of who Chase Reed really was.

He moved us back to the ledge by the ladder, and I watched as he climbed down first. Once he disappeared at the bottom, I shakily threw my leg over and climbed down, one careful step at a time—not looking beneath me. At the bottom, I considered kissing the ground, never so happy to be on solid ground before in my life. Maybe skydiving just wasn't in the cards for me. I guess time would tell.

Chase and I got to my room a little while later. I flicked on the light, relieved Chantel hadn't decided to cut her pledge bonding weekend short. I couldn't even begin to imagine what would've happened if she had returned early.

Chase sat down on my bed. "You gonna kick me off your bed this time?"

I crossed my arms and tilted my head, liking the look of him on my bed a hundred times more than I had that first time I found him on it. What a difference a little time made. "Depends."

He smirked. "On what?"

"Do you plan on pissing me off?"

He pushed himself to his feet and stalked toward me, cupping my cheeks between his hands. I quivered under his touch as he lowered his forehead to mine. "I told you I don't plan on doing a lot of talking." His mouth lowered to mine, his lips capturing mine in a delicious tangle of tongues. His hands slipped down my shoulders and over my arms before circling my hips and drifting to my ass. Without breaking our kiss, he lifted me right off my feet.

I hooked my arms around his neck and tightened my legs around his hips.

He turned and walked us to my bed. He lowered me down, following me and settling between my legs. I felt his kiss everywhere—hell, I felt *him* everywhere. Especially, between my legs. I deepened the kiss, arching into him as my hands skated down his muscular back. I wanted to be closer. I wanted the kiss to be deeper.

Chase finally pulled away, coming back up for air and leaving us both breathless. He studied my lips as our chests heaved liked we'd run a race. "You've clearly been kissed before. Why haven't you had sex?"

"Why have you?"

He laughed as his eyes lifted to mine. "Because it feels good."

My cheeks pulsed with heat. Why hadn't I anticipated that response? "Well…I'm waiting for the guy who'll make *me* feel good."

"I'm right here."

His words snagged my breath away—or maybe it was the honest way he said them. Because I knew he meant what he said. And that scared the living hell out of me.

He inched closer to me and our lips met again. The kiss started out slow and meaningful, but something inside me took over, and I needed to be closer to him. Our tongues and teeth fought for control as my hips sought friction. Understanding what I needed, Chase shifted his hips and his erection pressed between my legs. The pressure of his cock and the fabric of my jeans rubbing against my clit was too much.

A raspy groan escaped me, making Chase roll his hips as he kissed me. I may have been a virgin, but it didn't mean I'd never fooled around with a guy before and enjoyed it.

Eventually, Chase pulled back, his eyes riveting between mine. "Will you let me look at you tonight?"

My chest tightened, and a knot swelled in my throat, making it difficult to swallow. "Look at me?"

"I can't get the sight of you on the beach out of my mind."

I stifled a smile, loving that my plan to drive him wild had succeeded. I hadn't been able to get the sight of him on the beach out of my own mind either.

He sat back and reached for the top of my jeans. He raised his brows in question.

I nodded as my heartbeat accelerated.

Chase focused carefully as he slipped the button through the slot. He slowly pulled down the zipper, watching each tooth come apart. He grabbed hold of the hem of my jeans and looked to me for consent. I lifted my ass and he pulled the jeans down my legs and off my feet. He drank me in, his eyes sweeping slowly up my legs to my lacy pink panties.

I couldn't read the look in his eyes. Did he like what he saw or was he turned off that I didn't wear something skimpier like Chantel did?

Instead of driving myself crazy with what he may be thinking, I pushed myself up on my elbows and peeled my shirt over my head, tossing it to the floor.

Chase's eyes widened, taking in the matching pink pushup bra that gave me way more cleavage than I actually had. He swallowed hard. "Do you have any idea how beautiful you are?"

Tingles rushed up my arms, the hunger in his eyes and his words setting my body on fire.

He tried to lean forward to lay me back down, but I reached out and pressed my palm to his chest, stopping him. "What's wrong?" he asked.

"Your shirt's still on," I said.

His lips lifted into a sexy smirk. He reached behind his head and pulled it off, dropping it to the floor next to mine.

My fingertips skated across the front of his shoulders, so smooth and defined. He watched my hands as they explored his body, following them with his eyes as they ventured slowly down his chest. My thumbs flicked over his nipples before circling them. Chase's eyes drifted shut, reveling in the feel of my touch. My hands descended over his abs, tracing every deep ridge with the gentle touch of my fingertips. Holy hell he was so hot.

When he couldn't take anymore, he opened his eyes and lowered himself on top of me. "You gonna let me kiss you, Soph?"

"Since when do you ask?"

He leaned down, bringing his mouth to my ear. "Since I wasn't talking about your lips."

I sucked in a sharp breath before I nodded, eager for what came next.

He inched his way down my body, slowly tunneling his lips between my breasts.

My heart was pounding so fast, I was fairly certain he could feel it ready to burst through my chest.

He continued down, pressing soft kisses to my bare stomach. When he reached the elastic of my panties, his mouth hovered over me—keeping it a mere breath away from the lacy material. I inhaled sharply, holding in my breath as I waited for his lips to touch me, but only his warm breath moved over me.

I'd never wanted a guy's mouth between my thighs more than I did his in that moment.

But he didn't stop there.

I released my breath, feeling a little let down, until he whispered soft kisses down the inside of my left thigh. My body hummed to life, yearning for him there. Yearning for him *everywhere*. I struggled to decipher up from down when he was treating my body as carefully as he was, making sure not to miss an inch.

He reached my left foot, then moved to my right, dropping kisses all the way up from my ankle to my knee. He paused. I didn't need to peek. I knew what he was looking at. He lowered his lips to the small scars on my knee and peppered them with gentle kisses. I hated those ugly scars and what pain they'd caused me. But he was treating them with such care. It was as if, in that moment, he was helping me to let go of the painful reminder of my injury. Chase abandoned my scars and worked his way up the inside of my right leg. Once he reached the sensitive skin of my inner thigh, I pulled in another sharp breath, impatiently awaiting his next move.

His mouth hovered between my legs. "Has anyone ever kissed you here?"

"No," I breathed, unable to form any other coherent words.

"I promise you, it *will* feel good when I do."

"Do it," I urged.

He chuckled. "Not tonight."

I sighed, feeling my entire body deflate.

"Soon," he said as he trailed open-mouthed kisses across my stomach, licking a path around my navel. He worked his way up, tunneling his nose and lips between my breasts. "How about here?" He pressed kisses along the satin of my bra, gently licking under the seam of the cup. "Has anyone kissed you here?"

I nodded.

"Not like I will," he said.

A ripple rolled through my stomach. Was he trying to drive me wild so I willingly gave up my V card here and now? But if that were the case, why had he turned me down?

He brushed light kisses along my collarbone before reaching my mouth. But instead of kissing me, his lips lingered over mine, taunting me with their proximity. "When you're ready, I'll be read—"

I lifted my head and stole the words from his lips. My tongue pushed inside his mouth as I fought to gain the control he'd had. He deepened the kiss, tunneling his hands through my hair as he took over, setting the pace. His body began to move over me. His hips rolled again, his erection pressing once again between my legs, this time harder. The thin material left little barrier, and the sensations intensified. I wrapped my hands around him, my fingertips trailing up his back. It would be so easy to remove my panties and just let him show me how good it could feel. But at the same time, everything about us had been so screwed up. Who knew how he'd be acting tomorrow.

He finally pulled back, as both of us fought for air. "We've got time," he assured me.

I nodded, knowing he was right, but still reeling from everything he'd done to my body. Now I knew what it felt like for the guys I'd put the brakes on.

Chase rolled me onto my side so we lay chest to chest, facing each other. "We don't need to rush anything," he continued to assure me. He reached up and traced the outline of my lips.

I shuddered as the tip of his finger drifted from my lips to my left cheek and over my nose to my right cheek. "I love these freckles."

"Oh yeah?" I said, all breathless and still reeling.

He nodded. "You can't see them unless you're up close. Like they're a secret you only share with some people."

I closed my eyes, taking it all in. He *was* the guy in the media room. He *was* the guy who took me to the coast in a convertible. He *was* the guy I wanted to spend time with when he was acting like this.

"Will you tell me something?" he asked.

I opened my eyes only to be swept up in his pretty blue ones staring back at me. "What?"

"Do you ever plan to play soccer again?"

"Next question."

He hesitated, probably deciding if he should press me or not. "What else is in your jar?"

I smiled. "Lots of things."

"Give me a few."

I thought about the jar now hidden in the closet and all the private wishes I'd made for myself before starting here at Crestwood. "Get a tattoo."

"Yeah? What would you get?"

I shrugged. "Not sure. Something meaningful."

"I like that one. Tell me more."

"Oh…I don't know…normal college stuff… steal the school mascot…pull an all-nighter…watch the sun rise…skip a class."

"Skip a class?"

I shrugged. "I've never done it before."

He snickered. "What else?"

"Go to a fortune teller…have a picnic on the beach…go sledding on a dining hall tray."

"Not much snow in Texas."

"Stranger things have happened," I said, meaning more than just snow in Texas.

"They certainly have." He flashed me a lop-sided grin, reading my mind. "Does anything in that jar mention hooking up with a frat guy?"

"Absolutely not. Frat guys have STDs."

"I do think I've heard that somewhere before," he said, wrapping his arms around me.

I tucked my head beneath his chin as he held me to him. "But I think I do have one about falling asleep in a hot guy's arms."

"Are you calling me hot?" he asked.

"Maybe."

He laughed again.

That was one of the last things I remembered before sleep pulled me under.

CHAPTER TWENTY-TWO

The next morning, I woke with my arm and leg draped over Chase, who slept soundly beside me. I twisted instinctively to check Chantel's bed. It was empty. If she'd come back and found Chase and me in bed together, that would've been *very* bad.

I slowly pulled away from Chase and climbed off the bed, careful not to wake him. I grabbed his shirt from the floor and tugged it on, swiped my toothpaste and toothbrush from my closet shelf, and ducked out of the room.

When I returned from the bathroom, Chase sat on the edge of my bed, wringing his hands in front of him, his hair an adorable mess. He glanced up at me through his eyelashes. "I thought you bailed."

"And left you in *my* room? That would've been the worst move ever."

His eyes moved to the shirt I wore. "I like you in my shirt."

I glanced down at his shirt, which hung over my hands and down to my knees.

He crooked his finger at me.

I placed my toothpaste and toothbrush down on my desk and climbed onto his lap, straddling him.

"I have a confession to make," he said.

I stilled, preparing myself for the worst.

"I took a shot of your mouthwash."

"Yeah?"

He nodded.

"Does that mean you plan on kissing me?"

He nodded again, his dimples pinching the sides of his mouth.

I whispered. "Where?"

He reached his hand to the back of my head and drew my mouth to his, this time pulling my top lip between his and sucking on it gently. I waited him out as he moved to my bottom lip, doing the same. I closed my eyes, surrendering myself to his mercy. His tongue swept into my mouth, and only then did I join in, relaxing into him as he deepened the kiss, our tongues melding together.

His phone pinged somewhere nearby.

He reluctantly pulled back. "I'm sorry. I just need to check this." He reached for his phone on my desk and checked the screen. "Fuck."

"Something wrong?"

He paused, indecision flashing in his eyes. "I need to head home."

I felt everything inside me deflate. "Oh."

"Not home to the frat, home home."

"Oh." I climbed off his lap and leaned against my desk. "Is everything all right?"

He gathered his shoes and put them on. "Yeah. It will be."

Though the sight of him shirtless in broad daylight stole my breath away, I pulled off his shirt and handed it back to him.

Instead of taking the shirt, he grabbed my hand and pulled me to him, wrapping his arms around my waist as I stood between his knees in my bra and panties. He placed soft kisses to my bare stomach like he had the previous night. My knees weakened, and I hoped they didn't buckle. "I really don't want to leave."

"Then don't."

With a huff, he pulled back and took his shirt from my hand. I stepped back, and he pulled it over his head. "I really am sorry."

"It's fine. I had a nice time last night."

He quirked his brow. "Nice?"

"Very nice?"

"Oh, very nice." He smirked. "That's an improvement." He stood from my bed and wrapped his arms around me, pulling me into him one last time.

He lowered his nose and nuzzled it against mine before dropping a kiss to my lips. Regret shone in his eyes when he pulled away. He grabbed his backpack from my chair and went to the door, stopping before walking out. "If I'm not in class tomorrow, I'll try to give you a call."

"You don't think you'll be back?"

He shrugged. "I just never know." And then he was gone, disappearing into the hallway.

I fell onto my bed and inhaled deeply. Last night had been amazing. I just wished I wasn't waiting for the other shoe to drop.

* * *

Rain trickled down as Valerie and I ducked beneath our hoodies on our way to the dining hall for lunch.

"Do you know how bad I wanted to text you last night to hear what was going on?" she said.

I laughed. "You mean, you didn't come by and put your ear to the door?"

She laughed. "I thought about it." Her eyebrows bounced. "Did you guys…?"

I shook my head, not feeling like getting into the whole virginity thing. Sure, we were getting closer, but it wasn't something I openly discussed—unless provoked by an evil roommate.

"I've never seen him hold Chantel's hand," she said. "Or seek her out. *And,* the only time I've seen him show her any affection was that night you showed up thinking he sent the Uber."

"Seriously?"

"Oh, yeah. They were never touchy-feely. They were the complete opposite of how he was with you last night."

A strange sense of satisfaction washed over me as we made our way into the dining hall, shaking off the light rain that clung to our hoodies. We grabbed sandwich wraps and chocolate cake and found a table by the window.

"So?" she said.

"So what?"

"What *did* you do?" she asked.

I hesitated, unsure how much I wanted to say. "Well, when we left the party, we walked across campus."

Her brows furrowed, as if she wanted chocolate but got vanilla instead.

"It was nice," I said. "He brought me to the roof of one of the buildings. I think it was Salvador Hall. The one with the castle roof."

I watched her swallow down hard.

"Have you ever been up there?" I asked, before biting into my cake.

She shook her head, her eyes growing distant.

"He said they take their pledges up there."

Her eyes focused on the untouched vegetable wrap on her plate. "He shouldn't be talking about pledge stuff."

"Do the Alpha Phis do that?"

Her eyes flashed up, fear swirling in them.

"Did you have to stand on the ledge and recite *your* motto?"

Tears welled in her eyes. "Why are you asking me this?"

Aw, shit. What had I stumbled upon? I reached across the table and placed my hand over hers. "Oh, honey, you can talk to me. What's going on?"

She tugged her hand away. "Don't," she whispered. "People are always watching."

I glanced around the room. Some of her sisters were at a nearby table. While some of them were in the middle of conversations, others definitely looked our way. I looked back to her, speaking softly. "Did someone threaten you?"

"Please stop asking me questions." Valerie jumped to her feet. "I've gotta go."

"Valerie." I went to stand up.

"Stay here," she said through clenched teeth. "Just let me go."

"But—"

She spun away from me and hurried out the doors.

I glanced to the table filled with her sisters. All of them watched her go.

What the hell were they hiding?

CHAPTER TWENTY-THREE

Monday sucked.

One. Valerie had been ignoring my calls since lunch the previous day, *and* she wouldn't answer her door when I stopped by. Two. Chase didn't show up to History through Film. Nor had I seen or heard from him since he left my room yesterday morning. Three. Chantel returned while I was at class and cleaned out everything on her side of the room, apparently moving out. Actually, three wasn't so bad.

On Tuesday, I went to classes, received no calls or texts from Chase or Valerie, and ate alone.

"Hey, Sophia!"

I twisted around. Ryan jogged toward me outside the dining hall after my dinner alone. "Hi."

"Hey, so…I just wanted to explain what you saw Saturday night," he said, his eyes focused on his sneakers.

"What did I see?" I asked, completely confused.

He glanced up, lowering his voice. "In my room."

"What about your room?"

He cocked his head, his eyes examining my face. He had to see I had no idea what he was talking about. "Oh. I guess…you know what? Never mind."

"O-*kay*," I said.

"So, you and Chase?"

I shrugged, not really sure what to say.

"He's a good guy. But, good luck dealing with Chantel. That's gonna be a whole different story."

Wednesday, I threw my hair into a messy ponytail and trudged across campus toward History through Film. I'd never felt more alone. I wasn't the type to beg people to want to be with me, so I was waiting on Chase to call and Valerie to come around. But it didn't mean that it didn't hurt.

I entered class, stopping short in the doorway. The person coming in behind me bumped into me as I stopped. I glanced over my shoulder at her. "Sorry." I stepped into the classroom and moved down the aisle to my seat.

Chase sat in his seat, his eyes on his phone.

It took everything in me not to ask why he'd dropped off the face of the earth after leaving me on Sunday morning. But I pulled it together, sat down, and grabbed my laptop out of my bag.

"Hey," he said.

I didn't look at him. "Hi."

"How are you?"

I opened my laptop. "Peachy."

"So…" He began. "Friday?"

I opened a blank document on my computer.

"Valerie said it's your birthday," he explained. "Can I take you out?"

My eyes finally cut to his. "You spoke to Valerie?"

"Yeah."

"But, you didn't speak to me?"

He sighed. "I just ran into her."

"*Just* as in this morning or whenever you returned?" My eyes narrowed. "When was that by the way?"

"This morning."

I nodded, letting the knowledge settle.

"So, what do you say, Soph? Can I take you out?"

I tipped my head, studying his face. Did he really not understand my confusion—make that frustration? "Do you plan on disappearing between now and then?"

He dragged his teeth over his bottom lip as he thought about my question.

"Because I don't think I'm being unreasonable to just, I don't know, expect a phone call when you're on your way back so I at least know you're alive."

"Soph—"

"Look, I'm not trying to sound like a bitch. But I thought we came to an understanding Saturday night. But maybe that was just me thinking something was going on when it really wasn't."

He opened his mouth to respond.

"But I get it. You just got out of a relationship and you have family issues you need to tend to."

"I—"

"No need to explain. But if you don't mind, I've had a pretty shitty start to the week. Between you disappearing, Valerie ghosting me, and Chantel moving out, I really just need a break from the drama."

"Good morning, ladies and gentlemen," Professor Irons said as he walked into the room.

I turned to look at him.

"Your papers were fantastic," Professor Irons began. "The analogies you made between the two films as well as your keen eye to detail made them a pure pleasure to read. If you haven't checked the portal yet, your grades are in."

I pulled up the portal on my screen. I could sense Chase leaning in and looking over at my screen. Professor Irons' remarks read: *The A+ you deserved last time.*

"Nice job, Soph," Chase said, knowing I did the paper on my own after he ditched me for the second movie.

I didn't look at him. I needed time to figure out what to say. What to think. What to feel. There were so many red flags when it came to Chase Reed, and the fact that he hadn't apologized as soon as I walked in for his radio silence, told me he didn't get it.

Professor Irons released us early, so I gathered my things and stood up to go.

"So, what should we do Friday?" Chase asked as he followed me out of the classroom and down the hallway to the stairwell.

"I'm not really sure doing something's a good idea."

"Come on, Soph. Cut me some slack."

"Cut *you* some slack? Need I remind you that you just disappeared without a word for three days? And, how about our rocky start? How do I know those weren't all warning signs telling me this is a very bad idea?" I hurried down the stairs.

"You can't do that. You can't throw the past in my face. How are we supposed to move forward if you do that?"

I stepped outside and stopped to glare at him. "Is that what we're doing?"

He pulled me into his chest, wrapping his arms around me as people headed in all different directions around us. "I'm sorry."

Needing to see if his apology was sincere, I pulled my head back and looked up.

He looked down at me. "I've got shit to deal with at home that I don't talk about. It has nothing to do with you, so I try to keep that life and this life separate. Can I just ask you to be patient with me and not throw it in my face? I never meant to hurt you."

I stared into his eyes, so earnest and thoughtful. Ugh, I hated myself for being unable to resist his damn charm. "Will you ever be able to tell me what's going on at home?"

He nodded. "I just need time."

I thought about what he was asking. Could I give him time? Could I not ask questions or take things personally?

"What do you say?" he asked.

Damn you, dreamy blue eyes. I didn't want to be mad at him. But I also didn't want him to break my heart. And everything about him told me he'd break my heart. But being a glutton for punishment, I nodded.

He leaned down and captured my lips, kissing me slowly, like we had all the time in the world. I was lost in the kiss—not to mention his minty breath and rock-hard chest—when someone whistled, yanking me back to reality. We were standing in the middle of campus in between classes and people were moving all around us.

I pulled out of the kiss.

"Thank you, Soph. I won't let you down."

I turned and began walking.

He jogged to keep up. "Come by the frat tonight?"

"Why?"

"I missed you."

"I guess you should've called."

He laughed, knowing I wasn't letting that one slide. "Seriously. I wanna hang out."

"Is that right?"

He smirked, and when he smirked at me like that, I knew, come hell or high water, I'd be there.

CHAPTER TWENTY-FOUR

I lightly tapped on the front door of Kappa Sigma. I'd never been there when there wasn't loud music blaring from the windows and tons of people filling the rooms. But as I pushed open the front door, I found none of that. My footsteps creaked on the old wooden floor as I made my way into the house. A few guys played video games in the living room. But besides that, no one was around.

One of them glanced up from his game. "Who you looking for?"

"Chase."

"Try the basement," another said.

I walked to the basement door and made my way downstairs. Normally, bodies and spilled beer filled the dance floor. Now, it was just a big empty room.

Smack. Smack.

I looked around the basement and realized the sound was coming through an open door at the far end of the room that I'd never noticed before.

I moved toward it.

Smack. Smack.

I stepped into the open doorway and stilled.

Holy shit.

Chase, shirtless and sweaty, punched a punching bag that hung from the ceiling. He didn't notice me right away, so I watched him annihilate the bag, his fists relentless.

I knew he was built. I'd been privy to a front-row, show-and-tell session in my bed Saturday night. But this display of hotness and power was something else entirely. The sweat gave his muscles definition I hadn't noticed before. An X-rated vision of what I'd like to be doing with him pressed against me flashed through my mind.

"You gonna tell me what you're thinking about?" Chase asked.

I shook off the vision to find him standing there with his arms crossed. My eyes drank him in. "I…um…"

Dimples pinched into the sides of his mouth deeper than I'd ever seen them.

"Do you do this often?" *Stupid question.*

"Uh huh."

"So, you're a boxer in your free time?"

He smiled. "No, but I'd be a damn good one."

I walked into the room and straddled a nearby weight bench, awaiting more of the show. "Well, don't let me stop you."

He watched me settle onto the bench. "I didn't know what time you were coming over. I can go get showered."

"So soon?"

He stared at me, trying to figure out what I was getting at. Instead of beating the hell out of the bag some more, he walked over and straddled the weight bench so he faced me. "Hi."

"You're sweaty."

"Uh huh."

"I like you sweaty."

He threw back his head, and a mix between a humorless laugh and a groan escaped him.

"What?"

"Do you really think you can say something like that to a guy when you're sitting this close looking all hot and smelling all sweet?"

"Should I not have said it?" I asked, lifting my eyebrows.

"Oh, no. You should've. Just once we're alone in my room." He leaned forward and pressed his lips to mine. His sweaty nose brushed mine, and instead of being turned off by the beads of sweat shifting to my skin, I scooted closer, tunneling my fingers into the back of his damp hair and deepening the kiss.

Chase pulled out of the kiss. "Aw, fuck, Soph. Let's go up to my room." He grabbed my hand and pulled me to my feet. He led me upstairs and left me in his room so he could shower.

I sat on the edge of his bed, playing on my phone—anything to pass the time before his return. The vision of him in that basement with those glistening muscles pounding away at the punching bag overwhelmed me. I'd never been so turned on by just looking at a guy before, but there was something about Chase that made me want to throw caution to the wind and just enjoy the ride.

The knob on his door rattled a few minutes later and the door opened. Chase stepped through the doorway with a towel hung low around his waist, that distinct V carved into his hips, and water droplets clinging to his skin. "I figured if you liked me sweaty, you'd like me all wet," he said with a smirk, closing the door behind him.

I swallowed hard. *Damn straight I did.*

He moved toward the bed. My head tipped back to meet his gaze, all hooded and sexy. "What shall we do now?" he mused.

I placed my phone on his nightstand and slipped my hands over the towel at his hips.

His eyes dropped to my hands, waiting for my next move.

I trailed them slowly around to the front, slipping my thumb to where the towel was secured and loosening it. Chase made no move to grab for the slipping towel as it dropped to the floor.

My pulse began to thump as I slowly lifted my eyes from the towel on the floor to his erection in front of my face.

"Now what?" he asked, his voice deep and raspy.

I slowly met his gaze, having no idea what to do next. I mean I knew what I *could* do, but was that what I *should* do?

Gauging my indecision, he leaned forward until I had to lay back on his bed. I scooched up so my legs no longer hung off the side.

He covered me with his naked body and a drop of his wet hair landed on my cheek. He leaned down and licked it.

I smiled. "What shall we do now?"

"Oh, I know a lot of things we should do now," he said before his lips crashed down on mine.

My body fell slack, every part of me at his mercy. Or was I? I reached down between us and grabbed hold of his erection. Even as we kissed, he sucked in a sharp breath. I moved my hand over the thick length of him. He deepened the kiss, urging me on. I tightened my grip and pumped my fist up and down.

He tore his lips from mine and buried them in the crook of my neck, covering my skin with open-mouthed kisses that had my head falling back as I continued pumping my fist.

"Fuck, Soph," he said between kisses to my neck. "Where the hell did you learn how to do this?"

"I—"

"Wait, I don't want to know." His mouth captured mine, this time his tongue pushed inside and I could barely keep up. This kiss was hurried and desperate. And I hoped it was because of what I was doing to him.

I continued pumping my fist—faster and harder, doing whatever garnered a reaction from him. Sharp breaths were good. Groans were even better.

"Oh, fuck," Chase said, tearing his lips from mine and burying his mouth in my neck. He thrust into my hand as I continued moving. "Fuck, fuck, fuck *fuuuuuuuck*," he groaned as he spilled out onto my arm and hand as I continued pumping until I was sure I'd wrung his body of everything it had, bringing him over the edge completely.

I eventually released him.

He dropped his forehead to mine as his chest heaved. "That. Was. Amazing."

I smiled, satisfied with my work.

He rolled off of me and grabbed his towel from the floor. He wiped my arm and hand, then checked my clothes for anything that might have ended up on me. "Note to self. Seeing me in a towel gets you all hot."

"Don't make me go back to hating you."

He laughed as he stood from the bed.

I sat up, watching him go to his closet and pull on some jeans without boxers and a black T-shirt. He turned back to me. Instead of joining me on the bed, he walked to his door. "Come on."

"We're leaving?" I asked, suddenly confused by the turn of events.

"Nope. We're playing pool."

"Pool?" I asked, the sudden high pitch tone to my voice showing my surprise.

"You might've beaten Ryan, but there's no way in hell you're beating me."

Wait. What? "You saw us play?"

"Why do you think I was so pissed when I found you outside that night?"

"I have no idea."

He cocked his head, a sigh of resignation leaving his lips. "Because the second you kicked his ass in pool, I knew I'd never be able to stay away from you."

I sat speechless for a long moment, replaying his words and actions that night in my head, trying to make sense of them. "So, you decided to be mean to me?"

He walked over and lowered himself to his haunches in front of me, resting his hands on my thighs. "The asshole left you alone outside when you were clearly drunk. I was mad at *him*. And mad at *you* for putting yourself in that situation."

"*You* let me walk home alone."

He scoffed. "I followed you home."

My mouth parted. "I don't know if I should kiss you or add it to your list of creepy stalker tendencies."

He shook his head, not bothering with a response. "Then, you corrected me when I asked what you were doing out there. I knew then and there you were exactly what I wanted—but could never have. And it pissed me off."

I sat speechless, the newfound information whirling haphazardly through my mind. *He wanted me? But he thought he couldn't have me?*

"So, yes, Sophia. I saw you play pool. Are we clear now on what went down that night?"

"You could've just told me instead of being an asshole."

A bitter laugh escaped him. "I have a lot on my plate. Wanting you was not something I wanted to add to that plate." He reached up and brushed a rogue wave of my hair off my face and tucked it behind my ear. "But there you always were. In my classes. My history partner. Chantel's roommate. Ryan's latest obsession. It was like the universe telling me something."

"So, I was the reason for your bad attitude?"

He stood, grabbing my hand and pulling me to my feet. "You were the reason I smiled for the first time in a long freaking time and meant it."

Butterflies took flight in my stomach, his unexpected honesty flooring me. I had no idea how to respond. So, I said the first thing that came to my mind. "Care to wager on this game?"

His lips twitched in the corners. "What kind of wager?"

I thought for a moment. Then my mind wandered back to the sight of him in that towel. And I knew exactly what I wanted, especially since there was no way I'd lose.

CHAPTER TWENTY-FIVE

There was urgent knocking on my door Friday morning as I got ready for History through Film. I hoped Chase had decided to show up to surprise me. But when I pulled open my door, Valerie stood there holding a sign: *Happy Birthday, Sophia!*

I hadn't seen Valerie since she took off on me Sunday night. I knew I'd pushed too hard, and I understood that she wanted space from me. I didn't necessarily like it, but I respected it. So, this peace offering, especially on my birthday, meant the world to me.

Instead of saying anything, I stepped out into the hall and wrapped my arms around her.

She wrapped her arms around me, sign and all, hugging me back. "I missed you," she said.

"I missed you too."

* * *

I made my way to class a couple of minutes later. Once I neared the building, I stopped short and started cracking up. Chase sat outside the building on the front steps. His chest was bare and a white towel was wrapped around his hips. His eyes lit up with amusement once he spotted me, and he stood up to greet me as I moved closer to him.

Girls giggled and stared as they walked by, making me rethink my wager as I stepped in front of him. "I like your towel."

"I made a wager with the devil."

"Chantel was here?" I glanced facetiously around.

He enveloped me in his arms and dropped a kiss on my forehead. "Happy birthday."

"Thanks. Why are you out here? Are you trying to give the girls a show?"

"Only one girl." He stepped back and grabbed my hand, pulling me away from the building.

"What are you doing?"

"*We're* skipping class."

"Why?"

"It's on your list, so I'm making it happen," he said.

Heads turned as we made our way across the quad. "What are we gonna do?"

"Do you have something in mind?" he asked.

I thought about it for a minute. "Well, seeing you in that towel is reminding me of last night."

"I like the way your mind works," he said.

* * *

Chase held my hand as he drove through the busy streets of Houston that evening. I wore a sundress paired with a denim jacket and some nude heels Valerie lent me, hoping I hadn't overdressed for what he had planned.

"So, give me a clue," I said from the passenger seat.

He shook his head, his eyes on the road. "It's a surprise."

I sighed. "You're lucky I like surprises."

He glanced my way and smiled. "You're lucky I like you."

I laughed, watching out the window as the storefronts and restaurants blurred by us, knowing I didn't want to be anywhere but in that car with Chase. I glanced over at him, noting the way his shirt gripped his arms so perfectly. "Did you play football growing up?"

"Yeah, how'd you know?"

I shrugged. "You're just built like a wide receiver."

He laughed. "I *was* a wide receiver."

"Did you not want to play football in college?"

He opened his mouth to respond then closed it. "Just wasn't in the cards."

I got the strange feeling he was purposely being evasive, almost like he wanted to tell me but then thought better of it. "Did you have a lot of girlfriends?"

"This feels like an interrogation."

I squeezed his hand. "I just want to know you better."

"I had a few," he offered.

"No one serious?"

He shrugged. "How about you? No one waiting back home for you?"

I shook my head.

"Thank God. I would've had to kick someone's ass."

I laughed.

He eventually pulled into a parking lot.

I looked out the window at the small white house with beaded curtains hanging in the front window. My eyes lit up when I spotted the sign out front. I turned to Chase.

He grinned. "Check this off your list."

"This is awesome."

"Stay there," he said as he cut the engine and reached in the back for his ball cap. He put it on and hopped out of the car, making his way to my side. That brief moment gave me time to appreciate him in his dark jeans, light blue shirt, and ball cap pulled down low. He opened my door and took my hand, helping me out. He linked our fingers and we walked to the door. "Now if she says anything about getting rid of me, we're leaving."

I smiled, loving that he'd planned this for me.

We entered the front room and were greeted to soft tranquil music. A sofa was pushed against the far wall. There was a coffee table in front of the sofa with what looked like a crystal ball in the center. And another chair was in the corner.

"Welcome." An older woman sashayed into the room in a long colorful robe with rings on every finger. "You're here to have your fortunes told," she said with a thick Cajun accent.

"She's good," Chase whispered to me.

"Yes, I'm So—"

"Don't say anything, dear. Allow Madame Rose to tell you what you need to know. Come." She took my hand. "Let's read your fortune." She sat down on the sofa, pulling me down with her so our knees touched. She held my hand in her lap.

Chase sat across the room in the chair, stifling a smile.

"Madame Rose is sensing a milestone for you."

"Today's my birthday," I explained.

"Ah, yes. That's what I'm seeing. And you have some uncertainty surrounding the night."

I swallowed the lump that shot to my throat. Things had been heating up between Chase and me, and I had no idea where the night would lead us. "I—"

"You don't know what he has planned for you and you're curious," she said.

I glanced to Chase and nodded. "Very."

"I'm seeing big surprises in your future," she said. Then, something changed. Her mouth suddenly turned down in the corners and her features darkened. "But some of these surprises will come at a hefty price."

"Oh," I said, not quite sure what to make of her prediction.

"There are secrets. Lots of secrets being withheld from you…from various people in your life."

"Who?" I asked.

"Friends. A girl…and a boy. And…" Her head twisted toward Chase. "Him."

Chase pointed to himself. "Me?"

She nodded, her eyes narrowing on him. "Don't hurt the girl. She's got a tough exterior but a fragile heart."

His eyes widened, as if he was a small child being reprimanded for something he didn't do.

Madame Rose's attention moved back to me. "I also see happy things in your future, dear. A long life with a man who loves you and two children who are the apples of your eye."

I smiled, hoping that indeed was the truth and not just something she said at the end of a reading to send people away happy. "Do you see anything else I should know about?"

"Stay true to who you are and all roads will lead you in the right direction."

I pondered her words, even after we were in the car and pulling out of the parking lot.

"You're quiet," Chase said.

"That was intense."

"Do you believe what she said?" Chase asked.

"Well, if I did, I'd be asking you to drop me back off at the dorm since you're hiding a big secret."

He reached over and linked our hands. "Was it everything you thought it'd be?"

"And more."

We shared a laugh. "So, you ready for our next stop?"

I nodded. "Definitely."

* * *

"Keep them closed," Chase said as his car came to a stop.

My hands had been covering my eyes for the last ten minutes in the passenger seat. "They're closed."

He parked the car and switched off the engine. "Wait here."

"Where would I go? I can't see."

He opened his door and hopped out. I heard him open the back door and shuffle some things around.

"Can I open my eyes yet?"

"No." I heard the back door close then I felt my door being pulled open. "Keep your eyes closed," Chase said as he took one of my hands away from my eyes. "I want you to carefully turn and step out."

I did as told.

The crashing of ocean waves nearby brought a smile to my lips. A warm ocean breeze wafted our way, and I tasted the salt in the air on my lips.

"Why are you smiling?" he asked.

"Can't I just be happy?"

"Fine," he relented, knowing I'd discovered our location. "Open your eyes."

I did. We stood in the beach parking lot. Chase held a blanket, a box of pizza, another smaller white box, and two bottles of water. My smile grew.

"Come on." He led me to the path leading to the beach. Since the sun had set, very few people could be seen on the dark stretch of sand. Chase lay out our blanket and pulled me down with him. He wrapped his arm around me and pulled me into his side. "Happy Birthday, Soph. May this year be your best one yet."

"I can't see how it wouldn't be."

He pulled back to see my eyes. "Oh, yeah?"

"I've got straight As, a room to myself, and I met Val."

He frowned.

I couldn't hide my smile for long. "And, I met this guy, who continuously surprises me."

He smiled.

"Ryan."

He tackled me onto my back. "Ryan? You better take that back."

"Professor Irons?"

He growled.

"You, Chase Reed," I relented. "I met *you*."

He smiled. "That's better." He pressed his lips to mine for a quick kiss before sitting us back up.

I breathed in the briny night air as I reached for the pizza box.

"Nope," Chase said, as he reached for the smaller box and opened it. A big piece of chocolate cake sat inside. "Cake before dinner."

I cocked my head. "Valerie?"

He nodded as he handed me a fork.

I smiled, completely impressed by the lengths he'd gone to make my birthday one to remember. I dug into the cake and took a bite, savoring the fudgy taste.

"Does cake on the beach taste better than cake elsewhere?" he asked.

I shrugged. "I wouldn't have known until I tried it." I pressed my fork into the cake and held the bite-sized piece of cake out to him.

He leaned over and ate it.

"So, thanks for helping me check another thing off my list."

He pressed his lips to the side of my head. "I like making your wishes come true."

I smothered the grin fighting to take over. "Just tell me getting a tattoo isn't on the list tonight."

"Why?"

"Because not only does the idea scare the hell out of me, but I haven't figured out what I want yet."

"Fine. Not tonight. But this year."

I nodded. "This year."

* * *

We made our way down the hallway toward my dorm room a couple hours later. My nerves were in my throat. I wanted Chase to stay the night. I knew he was feeling serious about us. He was trying to make my wishes come true—and he wasn't pushing me to sleep with him. Which just made me want him more.

I punched in the code, and my door unlocked. I pushed it open and before I could switch on the light, I stilled, my eyes taking in the battery-operated candles placed all around my room.

Chase slipped his arms around me from behind and rested his chin on my shoulder, taking in the twinkling candles.

"You did this?" I said, my mind blown.

"I had a little help."

I spun in his arms and draped my arms over his shoulders. "Valerie?"

He nodded, his blue eyes extra clear with all the candlelight.

"This is one of the nicest things anyone has ever done for me."

He lifted a brow. "Nice?"

"Everything you've done for me has been amazing."

"I like amazing," he said, moving forward so I backpedaled into the room. I giggled as the door closed behind us and Chase leaned in, pressing his mouth to mine.

I arched into him and deepened the kiss, feeling it all the way down to my toes.

He pulled away much too soon and linked our hands, leading me to my bed. He sat first, pulling me onto his lap so my legs dangled off one side. "I haven't given you your present yet."

"There's more?"

He reached into his back pocket and pulled out a small black velvet pouch.

My heart fluttered. "What is it?"

He smiled. "Just open it."

I nodded, eager to see the contents. I reached my fingers inside and grasped something small and delicate. When I pulled my hand out, a sparkly silver necklace dangled from my fingers. I held it up so I could examine it, noticing the mason jar charm hanging on the chain. "Oh my God. I love it."

"I saw it and thought it was meant for you."

"Here." I handed it to him. "Would you put it on me?"

He took it from me and clasped it behind my neck, examining it on me. "Perfect."

"Hold on." I attempted to climb off his lap, but he held onto me. "I'll be right back," I explained. "I've got something for you."

"It's not my birthday."

I cocked my head, my silent plea to be released.

He relented.

I slipped off his lap and kicked off my heels, padding over to my closet and digging in the back. I unrolled the jeans where I had stashed my mason jar and walked back over to Chase.

He looked at the jar. The one he'd seen in the coffee shop that began his wish-granting mission.

I nudged him over. "Let's lay on my bed so I can show you."

He smirked. "I like where this is going."

He kicked off his shoes and we both sat against my pillows along the wall with our legs outstretched in front of us. I unscrewed the top of my mason jar and held it out to him. His brows shot up. "You sure?"

I nodded.

His eyes lit up as he reached in and pulled out a paper, unfolding it like a kid on Christmas morning. "Visit a fortune teller."

I plucked it from his hand and tossed it into the air. "Done."

He smiled as he pulled out another paper and unfolded it. "Have a picnic on the beach."

I plucked it away and tossed it to the floor. "Done."

He pulled out another. "Pull an all-nighter with a hot guy." He smirked. "You game?"

I nodded.

He placed that paper down beside him and pulled out another piece and unfolded it. "Go blonde." His eyes cut to mine. "Oh no you don't. I love your hair the way it is."

I smiled, loving how comfortable things between us had become.

He pulled out another piece of paper and unfolded it. "Lose my virginity." He stilled the second the words left his lips.

Nervous laughter escaped me. "Chantel wasn't lying. She definitely went through my jar."

"She had no right to," he said, folding up the paper and lowering it beside him.

A long silence passed between us.

"Is that a wish you're going to grant me tonight?" I asked.

He tipped his head, his eyes pleading with me. "*Soph.*"

"*Chase*," I mimicked.

"As much as I'm enjoying making your wishes come true, I don't want to rush you."

"You're not rushing me if I'm asking you to."

He scrubbed his hands up and down his face. "Listen, it's not easy being the gentleman in this situation because, I gotta tell you, I can't stop thinking about being inside you. How you'll feel and how you'll sound when I'm doing all the things I want to do with you. But…"

"I don't need you to be a gentleman. I just need you."

"Soph, being someone's first is a big responsibility."

I crawled onto his lap and straddled him, my knees on either side of him. "I'm twenty. I've waited to feel the way I feel when I'm with you. That can't be wrong."

He dragged his fingers through his hair, confliction written in every crease on his face.

I cupped his cheeks between my hands, the end-of-day stubble on his jawline prickling my palms. "I'm ready," I assured him.

He huffed, and I couldn't tell if it was out of frustration or waning control. He lifted me off his lap and threw his legs off the side of my bed.

Uh, oh.

I straightened my dress and sat back down where we'd been sitting. I stared up at him, feeling anxious, afraid he was going to turn me down.

He reached behind his neck and pulled his shirt over his head.

I released a slow shaky breath.

He walked slowly to the foot of my bed. I couldn't tear my eyes away from him as he grabbed hold of my ankles and pulled me down the bed so my feet hit the end and my back lay flat. I straightened my dress that had bunched up around my hips. He crawled his way over me, kneeling at my hips. He grabbed my wrists and lifted my arms over my head, holding them on the pillow with one hand. "I'm gonna need you to stay still."

My eyes widened unsure what he intended to do.

"Now, I don't want to do anything you're not ready for, but hell, it's getting difficult to be alone with you and not touch you."

I swallowed my nerves.

"Will you let me touch you?"

I nodded.

"Down there?"

More anxious than I'd ever been in my life, I nodded.

"I'm not pressuring you, right?"

I shook my head.

His hand released my wrists and he slowly peeled my dress up and over my raised arms, revealing my lacy black bra and tiny black thong. He hissed his pleasure as he tossed my dress to the floor. "God damn."

Goosebumps raced across my skin.

"No matter what I do, I want your hands up there."

"Don't you trust me?"

"I don't trust *me*," he said with no hint of humor in his tone. He lowered himself onto his side beside me. My heartbeat quickened as his hand slipped under the elastic on my panties, sliding down between my legs. My eyes pinched shut and my head pushed back into the pillow as one of his fingers dipped inside me. My back arched off the bed, unprepared for the shock of his touch. He removed his finger and slipped it along my folds. I shuddered as he found my clit, circling it with his finger. I moaned softly as tingles built.

His lips lowered to the sensitive skin beneath my ear and he pressed open-mouthed kisses to my neck.

He circled my clit with his thumb while two fingers dipped inside me. I arched off the bed again.

"You okay?"

I nodded.

"Is this good?" he asked.

"God, yes."

He chuckled before pressing more kisses up and down my neck. And, instead of pumping his fingers inside me, he slid them over my folds, his thumb applying pressure and circling my clit until my entire body tightened like a coil. I gasped quick short breaths as my body threatened to let go. I tried to hold on. Tried to let the feelings build. But, he kept circling, around and around. I couldn't concentrate. I lost all focus. And, all at once, the coil released, sending tingles rippling out to every part of my body. My entire body trembled, but he didn't stop circling, milking every last tremor out of me as I rode out the most amazing orgasm I'd ever experienced.

"God, I love watching you let go like that," he murmured.

"Stop talking," I said, with my eyes still closed and my body a livewire.

He laughed. "Have you done that before?"

When I finally came back down to earth and dragged in as many breaths as I could muster, I opened my eyes to find him inches away from my face.

"Only with myself."

He jerked back with wild eyes. "Do you have any idea how hot that is?"

I stared at him, still very much reeling from the experience of having an orgasm with someone else.

"Will you let me watch you?"

"If I decide to see you again after tonight? Maybe."

He wrapped his arms around me and rolled onto his back, pulling me on top of him. "If you decide to see me again? Were you just using me?"

I finally lowered my arms and slipped them around him, hugging him to my chest. "Maybe," I teased.

"Well, just so we're clear. I'm not going anywhere. And, we've got all the time in the world to do other stuff."

I wouldn't lie and say I wasn't disappointed because I was completely disappointed, but if I believed his words—believed we had the time he was offering—there was no rush. "This has definitely been my favorite birthday."

"And it's not even over yet. We still need to pull an all-nighter. And there are a lot of other things we can do."

A rush of excitement filled me. Why had I been so let down when I knew for a fact that he had a great imagination when it came to making me feel good.

And by five in the morning, with our eyelids threatening to close, we'd done a number of things I'd never done before. And, while losing my V-card may not have been one of them, it didn't make my day any less spectacular.

CHAPTER TWENTY-SIX

I stood outside the gym entrance Monday afternoon, watching the people coming and going in workout clothes. As instructed by the mysterious text Chase had sent earlier, I wore shorts and a T-shirt and hoped my reaction to seeing him annihilate that punching bag had given him an idea that included me and some workout equipment.

"Soph."

I spun around.

Chase approached in basketball shorts and a T-shirt, turning heads as he walked to me.

"Hey. What's going on?" I asked.

He stopped in front of me, pressing a kiss to my lips. "Okay. Don't kill me."

My eyes widened, almost afraid to ask.

He ticked his head to the side. "Follow me."

We didn't enter the gym but rounded the building until we stood in a grassy area behind it. The vast area, separated by chain-link fences, was filled with fields. Baseball to the far right. Football to the left. And a soccer field in the center with its freshly mowed green grass and freshly-painted white and yellow lines. A couple of people—I assumed coaches—stood by the goal talking.

"One of my frat brothers volunteers for the girls' soccer team," he explained.

I froze, my heart beginning to thump in my chest as I stared out at the field. "What did you do?"

"He said the team sucks. They're D3 and haven't won a game yet this season."

"What did you do?" I repeated.

"I got you a tryout with the coach."

I spun back to face him. "A tryout?" All the reasons that was an insane idea whirled through my mind. "I haven't played in a year and a half."

"So?"

"I don't even have cleats."

He smiled, probably pleased I was more concerned with my lack of cleats than hauling off and punching him. "So?

"I don't even know if..." my voice trailed off, not wanting to say what I was really thinking.

He grabbed my shoulders and ducked his head to meet my eyes. "You *will* be good enough."

I closed my eyes, pained by the idea of stepping on a soccer field again after such a long absence.

"Don't let the fear of failing be the reason you don't do something you love."

I opened my eyes, unsure if I was pissed he'd gone behind my back or overjoyed that he'd do something like this for me.

"It's just a tryout with the coach," he assured me. "She just wants to see what you're capable of. When she heard you were going to play D1, she wanted you on the team without even seeing you play."

"I *was* going to play D1. I have no idea what I'd be able to play now."

"You won't know until you try."

I pulled in a deep breath. Could I still play? Would I just be embarrassing myself if I tried out and didn't make it?

"If nothing else, you'll know the truth," he said. "If you still have what it takes, then next year when you're eligible, you'll have a spot on the team."

I tugged the hairband off my wrist and pulled my hair back into a ponytail, knowing this moment could affirm my fears or prove me wrong.

Boy, I sure hoped it proved me wrong.

* * *

An ice bag rested on my knee as I lay on my bed that night. To say my knee was sore would be an understatement. Since I hadn't been using my knee in that capacity in over a year, it had been super tight during the impromptu tryout. Luckily, it wasn't tight enough that I couldn't show the coach what I could do with a soccer ball.

Though I'd be ineligible to play on the team this year because I was a transfer student, the coach offered me a spot on the team next year, and I accepted.

Knowing my knee was sore, Chase had given me a piggyback ride back to my dorm. The whole way back he told me how awesome I looked and promised to massage my knee whenever I needed him to. That might prove to be more often than not seeing as though I agreed to begin practicing with the team starting next week.

Chase had been right.

I'd been letting my fear of failing hold me back. But the second I had that soccer ball at my foot, I knew playing soccer was what I needed to be doing to make me feel like me again. It was the one thing that had been missing from my life, and I hadn't even realized how much until that moment.

Someone banged on my door, pulling me from my thoughts.

I removed the ice bag and stood from my spot on my bed, approaching the door. "Who is it?"

"Valerie."

I pulled it open, and Valerie stood there with tears staining her cheeks. "Oh my God. What's wrong?"

She walked into my room and dropped down on Chantel's bare bed, holding her phone out to me. "I'm getting kicked out of school."

"What?" I closed the door and moved to her, taking her phone and pressing the video on the screen.

"Stand still, pledges!" Valerie yelled at a row of pledges whose faces had been blurred.

The camera zoomed in on the pledges' nearly naked bodies which had been circled in black marker in various places.

"Let's go sisters!" Valerie yelled as she paced back and forth in front of the pledges, tapping the areas on their bodies with a yardstick that had yet to be circled. "You missed lots of fat here!"

I switched off the video, unable to stomach this cold version of Valerie on the screen. "That didn't even sound like you."

"Do you hate me?" she asked.

"Why'd you do it?"

"That was last semester's pledge class. Chantel made me do it."

"No one makes you do something like that. Especially, if you don't want to do it."

We both fell silent. I wondered why she was showing the video to me. Had other people seen it? Is that why she was being kicked out of school?

"During hell week," Valerie sniffled. "Pledges are barely allowed to sleep."

"I've heard that."

"And they have to do all sorts of crazy things while they're sleep-deprived."

"Like allow sisters to circle their body fat?"

"That's not even the worst of it." She paused as if she didn't wholeheartedly want to tell me what she was about to tell me. "They have to tell their deepest, darkest secret."

"Did you have to do that as a pledge?"

She paused for a moment, then nodded.

"And Chantel records the secrets, amongst other incriminating things, as you've seen."

"Why?"

"So, if any of us step out of line or do anything she thinks looks bad for the Alpha Phis, she'll expose us."

I suddenly understood why everyone always tread so lightly around Chantel. One wrong move and their unsavory behavior or deepest secret would go viral. The juicier the secret, the greater fear instilled in her "sisters."

I waved her phone out. "Who's seen this?"

"I'm sure everyone by now, including the dean."

"So, why'd she leak it?" I asked.

Valerie cocked her head as if I should already understand.

My eyes widened. "Because of me?"

"What was it she said?" Valerie asked. "Payback's a bitch?"

"That was directed at *me*."

"By releasing the video, she hurt both of us. She knows we're close. If I get kicked out, you lose a friend."

"And if you don't get kicked out?"

"Well, then, she's making sure I won't tell you things."

"What kind of things?"

She shook her head, scared of whatever it was she wasn't saying.

I knew better than to push her. When I'd pushed her, she'd disappeared.

I pressed my palms to my eyes as guilt flooded my body. "So, this was a warning?"

She nodded. "To both of us."

"I'm so sorry."

She shook her head, not looking for an apology or my sympathy. "It could've been my secret," she said. "The hazing's nothing compared to my secret." Her eyes moved away from mine. "And she knows it."

"What's that mean?"

She looked back to me, her eyes lifeless and dark. "Another wrong move and it's out there."

CHAPTER TWENTY-SEVEN

"I saw Valerie cleaning up leaves on the quad earlier," Chase said.

I peeked up at him seated across from me in the coffee shop. "At least she's still here."

Valerie had been called to the dean's office to discuss the video that surfaced. I don't know what she said to the dean, but he decided not to kick her out of school. However, she was placed on probation and sentenced to one-hundred hours of on-campus community service. So, her free time no longer belonged to her. I'd offered to help her, seeing as though I was partly to blame for Chantel's payback, but she wouldn't allow it.

But I still couldn't shake the guilt I felt.

"When do you wanna watch the movie?" I asked Chase.

"You tell me. Because you alone in a dark room is all the motivation I need."

"We actually have to get our paper written."

He rolled his eyes. "So demanding."

I bunched up a napkin and tossed it at his face.

He laughed, the raspy sound burrowing into every crevice around my heart as he grabbed it from the table where it bounced.

Oh, man. I was more far gone than I ever imagined.

"So, she makes the soccer team, and all of a sudden she thinks she can start ordering me around?" He tossed it back at me, but I caught it in the air.

"Ordering you around?" I laughed. "Oh, the irony,"

"Well, isn't this nice."

Our eyes jumped to Chantel, standing beside our table with her hands dug into her hips.

Her eyes moved to mine. "Just saw Valerie cleaning up leaves. I wonder what made her go all crunchy earthy these days?"

I shoved back my chair, prepared to get in her face, but Chase grabbed my arm, stopping me from standing.

Chantel's eyes dropped to his hand on me. "Watch him. One minute he doesn't have time for a relationship, the next he does. Seems like he doesn't know what he wants."

I tried reining in the anger I felt toward her. How could she hurt Valerie the way she had? Especially since it was me she was really angry at. "How could you do that to her?"

"Do what?" Chantel asked, all innocent and perplexed.

Heat rushed to my cheeks. "Next time you want payback, I'm right here." I jumped to my feet, this time too fast for Chase to stop me from standing. He grabbed my arm as I stood there, stopping me from touching her.

Her eyes cut to Chase, ignoring me entirely. "I hope you haven't slept with her yet. I'll never take you back if you have."

"Take him back?" I said. "You're as crazy as you are cruel."

"He likes the chase. You made it too easy. He'll get bored."

"I'm sitting right here," he said. "And you don't know a thing about me and Sophia."

"You're right. I don't. Because I never thought the two of you would stab me in the back the way you have." She spun away from us and marched out of the coffee house.

I dropped back into my seat, my entire body trembling with anger.

"Don't let her get to you."

I scoffed. "Why'd you hang out with her for so long?"

"I'm a guy. We do stupid stuff."

"Was it for the sex?"

He tipped his head.

"*What?* It's a valid question."

His eyes drifted off, and I wondered if I'd made him angry for asking. "Chantel and I never had sex."

"*Right.*"

His eyes moved back to mine. "I'm serious. We may have fooled around, but that was it."

"Like us?"

"Nothing like us."

"What's the difference?"

He jerked a glance over his shoulder, taking in the busy coffee shop. "Are we really doing this here?"

I shrugged. "Seems timely."

He released a breath. "You're real. You're honest. You like me for me and not what I look like standing next to you."

"*Wellllll,*" I teased, pretending the last one wasn't entirely true.

He laughed. "You know what I mean. I can be me with you and laugh with you. And I know you're being the same with me."

I reached for the necklace he'd given me and slid my finger up and down the chain. He'd been right about Chantel and me. We couldn't have been any more different.

Thank God.

CHAPTER TWENTY-EIGHT

Chase's name appeared on my screen as I walked back from my last class on Friday. I lifted my phone to my ear. "Hey."

"Soph?" The rushed tone of his voice told me something wasn't right.

"What's wrong?"

"I need you to make me a promise."

My brows tugged together. "What?"

"Do not go to the frat tonight."

I stopped in the middle of the path as students walked around me. "Why?"

"I just need you to trust me."

"Okay."

"Okay, you won't go?" he confirmed.

"You asked me not to go and to trust you. And I do." Silence filled his end.

"Chase?"

"Yeah."

"Are you okay?"

Silence.

What the hell?

"I will be," he finally said. "I'll call you later."

He had to know asking me not to do something was going to pique my curiosity. I needed more information than he'd given. But I'd do what he asked even if I didn't understand it. "Okay."

"I love you, Soph."

My thoughts ground to a halt as goosebumps scampered up my arms.

"You there?"

"Um…I'm here. I'm just…"

"I just wanted to be sure it was said. I gotta go." He disconnected the call and was gone.

What. The. Hell?

* * *

I lay on my bed staring up at the ceiling. I'd checked my phone a hundred times between the time Chase dropped the L word on me and now. I knew how I felt about him, but the L word was a huge step. Was he mad that I hadn't said it back? Did he think I didn't care about him the way he cared about me?

My phone rang.

I grabbed it without even checking the number. "Hello?"

"So…ph…ia?"

"Val?"

"I ne…ed y…ou," she slurred.

I sat up. "Are you drunk?"

"I th…ink some…thing was…in…my dr…ink."

Alarm bells wailed in my head. I jumped to my feet and shoved my feet into my shoes. "Where are you? I'm coming."

"Kap…pa Phiiii."

I stilled. Chase asked me not to go there tonight. "Is Chase there?"

"I…dun…nooo."

"Ryan?"

"Ya."

"Can you get to him?"

Silence.

"Val. I'll be there as fast as I can. Stay on the line." I threw open my door and ran down the hallway. I made it down the three flights of stairs in record time and flew outside. I held the phone to my ear as I jogged as quickly as I could across the dark campus. I knew I needed to call 9-1-1, but I couldn't risk hanging up with Val. "Talk to me, Val. Who did this?"

Silence.

"Val?" I nearly screamed.

"He...re."

I heaved a sigh of relief. "Do not go anywhere with anyone. You scream if anyone tries to get you alone."

"I th…ink I'm in…. 's..."

"You cut out, Val. Where are you?"

Silence.

I turned the corner to the main road. I could see Kappa Sigma's front porch and black shutters, now looking more ominous than ever before. "I'm almost there, honey, stay with me."

My lungs burned and my knee felt tight as I bolted up the walkway and threw open the front door. Music blared from the speakers on the main floor, pounding as fiercely as my heartbeat. People packed the hallway and rooms. My head whipped from side to side, seeking out Valerie, but I couldn't find her among all the unfamiliar faces.

I ran to the basement, stopping on the top step and scanning the faces of those who danced on the dance floor. I spotted Tina, but no Val.

I turned and hurried to the main staircase leading up to the second floor. I took two steps at a time and threw open the first closed door on the right, barging in on a couple going at it on the bed. "Oops. Sorry."

I spun around and hurried across the hall, throwing open that closed door and barging in. The room was empty. I moved to the next room. My hand landed on the doorknob.

"Police!" a voice shouted downstairs.

Screams were accompanied by the shuffling of feet pounding on the floor beneath me. I ignored the noise and twisted the door handle. Locked. I pounded on the door. "Val! Are you in there?"

Nothing.

The noise on the main floor grew louder as people scrambled to exit the house and avoid the police. Ignoring the commotion, I moved to the room across the hall. I turned the handle and it too was locked. I pounded on the door. "Val, if you're in there, yell!"

I spotted Ryan's room next door. I hurried to it, twisting the knob and pushing open the door.

I froze. The hair on the back of my neck stood on end and a cold chill rushed up my spine.

Val lay on the bed completely naked with Ryan seated beside her, fully clothed.

"Oh, thank God you're here," I said to him as I rushed over and threw a blanket from his chair over Valerie. "Someone drugged her."

He jumped up. "Oh. Yeah. That's what I thought."

The pounding of footsteps on the staircase told me it was just a matter of time before the cops made it to us.

"Do you know who did it?" I asked Ryan as I leaned over Valerie to be sure she was breathing. She was.

"No idea."

"Did you call 9-1-1?"

"Hands where I can see them!"

Ryan spun around with his hands raised.

"Thank God you're here," I said, my eyes cutting toward the door. "She's been drug—" My words were cut off by the sight of Chase, in a black bulletproof vest, with a gun pointed at Ryan. His eyes were on mine and a thousand thoughts played across his face. Seconds felt like hours before he tore his eyes away from mine and spoke into the walkie on his shoulder. "We need a medic sent to the second floor." He moved toward Ryan. "Turn around and put your hands behind your back."

"Fuck you," Ryan spat.

Chase whipped handcuffs off his belt and twisted Ryan around so his chest hit the wall.

"I can't believe you're a fucking cop," Ryan said.

Chase grabbed Ryan's wrists behind his back and snapped on the cuffs. "You don't know how long I've wanted to do this."

My eyes shot daggers at Chase. "What are you doing? Valerie was drugged and he helped her."

He glanced at me over his shoulder. "He's the biggest dealer on campus." He spun Ryan away from the wall so he faced the door. "I have a feeling he's been drugging girls for quite some time."

My eyes shot to Ryan who kept his eyes down. "Did you do this?"

He didn't look at me or say anything.

I jumped up and circled in front of him. "DID. YOU. DO. THIS. TO. HER?!?"

He forced his eyes up. They were cold and detached.

I lifted my hand and smacked him across the face, the *thwack* echoing through the room. I spun around and hurried back to Val, holding her hand and telling her it was gonna be all right as my entire body shook with fear, anger, and confusion.

Two more officers entered the room.

"Take him downstairs," Chase told them.

The taller officer grabbed Ryan by the arm and marched him out of the room.

"Is the medic on his way?" Chase asked the other officer.

The officer nodded before walking over to Valerie and checking her vitals.

"Is she gonna be okay?" I asked him.

"The EMTs will be here any second," he said before leaving the room.

"I told you not to be here," Chase said through gritted teeth, his eyes burning into mine.

"Why? So, you could keep lying to me?"

"You have to know I couldn't tell you," he said.

More officers entered the room with two EMTs.

"What happened?" one of the EMTs asked me.

"She was drugged. That's all I know."

As they took her vitals, I searched the room for her clothes which were folded on Ryan's dresser. I'd been in Valerie's room enough times to know she never folded her clothes. That snake. My eyes welled up as I grabbed the clothes. "I'd like to go with her."

The EMTs nodded as they moved her onto a stretcher.

I avoided Chase's gaze as I moved out of the room by Valerie's side. She needed me.

CHAPTER TWENTY-NINE

Valerie's heart monitor beeped monotonously as I sat in the chair beside her hospital bed. She'd been unconscious since we arrived, though the nurses assured me she'd be coming out of it soon. I checked my phone for the time. Three in the morning. And Chase still hadn't called.

I guess I wasn't surprised.

Nothing pertaining to him—or Ryan for that matter—could surprise me now.

How had I been so blind?

He hid a major part of his life, and I fell for his deceit—his facade—hook, line, and sinker. He must've thought I was so stupid. So naïve. Why hadn't I believed Madame Rose when she said there were secrets being withheld from me? She even warned me about Chase and I didn't believe her.

Sitting at Valerie's bedside had given me time to think. Time to replay every moment with Chase. Every interaction. Every promise he made to me. But none of it added up to anything real. Anything tangible I could grasp onto. It had all been a lie. A grand manipulation to bring down the college drug dealer.

"Sophia?" Valerie whispered.

"Val?" Though her eyes were barely cracked, I leaned in so she could see me. "Are you okay?"

"Thank…you," she whispered.

"I'm just happy you're awake. Let me get the nurse."

"I'm so tired. I just need to sleep."

"Sleep. I'll be right here. I promise. You can't get rid of me even if you try."

"BFF," she whispered.

Tears glossed my vision. "Sleep."

The soft purrs leaving her told me she'd already fallen asleep.

I stood from my chair and walked out into the hallway. The sterile bleach stench hit me as I walked to the nurse's station.

The nurse on duty glanced up from her computer station.

"Valerie just woke up."

"Is she in any pain?"

"She said she was tired and then fell back asleep."

"Then let her sleep. Her body needs it."

I nodded.

"I'll check on her in a little bit," she assured me.

"Thank you." I returned to Valerie's room and dropped into the hard chair I'd been in since arriving. The intensity of the night, mixed with the emptiness occupying my chest, was too much for me to handle. I curled into a ball in the chair and rested my head on my knees. I closed my eyes and prayed that sleep would pull me under. And maybe then, after I woke up, I'd find it was all just a terrible dream.

* * *

"Sophia?"

My head jolted up. My eyes whipped around, trying to grasp where I was. White walls. Beeping machines. Valerie in a hospital bed. *Dammit.* "Are you okay?" I asked, my groggy voice sounding nothing like my own.

"I think so," she said. "What happened?"

"You were drugged."

She nodded. "I know. I called you, but then I don't know how I got here."

"An ambulance."

"Did everyone see?" she cringed, clearly embarrassed by the idea of being taken out of a party on a stretcher.

"The cops pretty much cleared the house before you were even taken out."

"The party got broken up?"

With a deep exhalation, I nodded. "Something like that. Do you know who drugged you?"

She shook her head.

"The cops think it was Ryan."

Her lips twisted regrettably, as her eyes dropped away from mine. "I had a bad feeling."

I shook my head, so blindsided by the news and angry that I hadn't hit him harder. "He was alone with you in his room."

She gasped.

"I'm pretty sure I got there before anything happened."

Tears pooled in her eyes.

"Oh, Val. Don't cry. You're safe. He got arrested."

"He did?"

I nodded. "Chase arrested him."

Her face fell. "Oh my God, *what?*"

A nurse walked in. "You're up," she said with a smile, pulling our attention from one another. "How's the head?" she asked as she checked Valerie's monitors.

"Banging like a drum," Valerie admitted.

"That's to be expected." She frowned. "I'm going to have to administer a rape kit on you."

Valerie quickly looked to me.

I nodded. "You need to, Val. Just to confirm what we already know. Nothing happened."

"Okay," she said to the nurse.

"And," the nurse hesitated, not wanting to say what she clearly had to say. "There are two officers here who'd like to speak to you."

Unexpected dread crept into my body.

"Would it be okay if I let them in?" she asked. "Or do you want me to tell them to come back later?"

Valerie's eyes cut to mine again in question.

I nodded. "Let's get this over with."

The nurse walked out into the hall.

Valerie looked to me. "Did you know he was a cop?"

I shook my head. "I'm as shocked as you."

A uniformed police officer stepped through the door. I breathed a sigh of relief. Then, Chase in jeans and a black Henley stepped into the doorway and followed him into the room.

My eyes dropped away, suddenly realizing where he'd been all the times he'd disappeared. He'd been meeting up with his unit. He had this whole other life I had no knowledge of. *Oh my God.* Did he have a girlfriend? A wife? Bile inched up the back of my throat and I jumped to my feet. "I'll be back," I mumbled to Valerie as I scurried out of the room with my eyes on the floor.

I stepped into the hallway and closed my eyes, dragging in deep breaths.

"You okay, honey?" a nurse asked.

I nodded. "I'm fine." But I wasn't. Not even close. Chase hadn't tried to call. He hadn't tried to explain. It was clear I'd been part of the job. Part of the elaborate farce. And now he had no use for me.

Despite my broken heart, I needed to be there for Valerie. So, pulling in a breath and steeling my features, I walked back into the room.

All eyes shifted to me, but I kept mine on Valerie as I dropped back down into the chair.

"So, you didn't see him slip anything into your drink?" the officer asked.

Valerie shook her head.

"But he gave you an open container?" Chase asked.

She nodded.

"How soon after did you start feeling groggy?" Chase asked.

"Almost immediately because I hadn't had anything to drink up to that point. Then, my pulse started to race. I felt fidgety and sweaty. I knew something wasn't right, so I called Sophia." She looked to me. "Thank God she showed up when she did."

I reached over and took her hand, holding it between mine.

"Has this ever happened to you before at Kappa Sigma?" the officer asked.

Valerie shook her head. "But I have heard other girls say they woke in guys' beds with no recollection of how they got there. They just thought they were wasted. But now I don't know."

Chase shook his head and I could see he was angry. "I'm sorry I let this happen," he said. "If I'd had solid proof sooner, my unit could've moved in and taken him down before you got caught up in his twisted game," he explained.

Valerie shook her head. "You got him now."

"If you remember anything else that might help us bring more charges against him, please don't hesitate to call me or Officer Shaw," the police officer said, placing his card down on the table beside Valerie's bed.

Shaw? Chase's last name was Shaw? Was his first name even Chase?

They turned and walked toward the door. The officer exited, but Chase stopped.

My chest tightened around my racing heart.

He glanced over his shoulder at Valerie. "I'm glad you're all right." He turned and walked out of the room without even looking my way.

Valerie squeezed my hand. "Don't cry."

"I'm fine."

"You're not."

"*You're* in the hospital. I'm going to be okay."

"You two need to talk," she said.

"His last name's Shaw. He's a cop. I didn't know either of those things." I closed my eyes. "He's probably married with kids. No wonder why he wouldn't sleep with me." I dropped my face into my palms. "This was his job. *I* was just part of his job."

Valerie remained silent for a long time so I peeked up to be sure she was okay. She stared at me, the dark circles around her eyes reminding me of the horrific night she'd had and what could've gone wrong if I hadn't gotten to her in time. "I don't believe you were just part of his job. I saw him with you. He was different. He had me decorate your room with candles for God's sake. You don't do romantic stuff like that if you're faking it."

I shook my head, tears stinging my eyes. "This isn't really helping."

She flashed a sad smile. "I'm sorry."

"No, I'm sorry."

We both laughed, but it didn't feel like real laughter as we considered the sad situations we were both in at that moment.

But we were strong.

And, we had each other.

We'd move past this.

CHAPTER THIRTY

I sat alone in the coffee shop on Friday afternoon, trying to ignore the hollow in my chest that had been there since Saturday night. I wrote my History through Film paper alone. *Alone* because my partner was no longer a student at Crestwood. *Alone* because my partner lied to me about everything. *Alone* because my partner didn't care enough about me as a human being to even talk to me after deceiving me.

Some girls at a nearby table spoke in whispers. I could've sworn I heard them say something about the campus NARC. And when my eyes shifted to them, they lowered their voices even more.

My stomach turned over, my thoughts never straying far from the grand deception I had my very own front-row seat to. What was it going to take to move on?

"Well, looks like neither of us ended up with him," Chantel said, stepping up to my table.

"Instead of gloating, I'd think you'd be asking how Valerie is? You know Valerie. Your sorority sister."

She rolled her eyes. "It's not like it's the first time she ended up in someone's bed."

"Wow. If that's how you talk about your friends, I can only imagine how you talk about me."

She scoffed. "I don't."

I knew that was a lie. She wasn't someone to let things go. She dwelled on them. She made people pay for them.

And that's when it hit me.

The distance between her and Val. Their strained interactions. The fear she instilled in my usually confident and strong friend. "Oh. My. *God.*"

"What?" she sneered.

"Did you set her up?"

"What?"

"Did you have Ryan slip something in her drink? Was this more payback like the video?"

She straightened her spine. "I have no idea what you're talking about."

"I think you do. Jesus Christ. It's all starting to make sense now."

"You have no idea what you're talking about."

"Oh, but I do."

When it hit her that I might actually know something, her eyes narrowed and her face contorted into something cold and calculating. "You have no idea who you're dealing with."

"You're wrong about that too. I do. And I'm not scared of you."

"You should be." She spun around and walked out, the clicking of her heels drumming in my head like my own pulse.

I gathered my things. How had I not seen it before now? I left the coffee house and jogged back to the dorm.

I knew why they didn't get along.

I knew Valerie's secret.

And something needed to be done about it.

CHAPTER THIRTY-ONE

My heart had been racing. But when the knock on the door came, it became a jackhammer in my chest. I glanced over at Valerie who sat on my bed, her hands wringing nervously in front of her. She nodded her permission.

I walked to the door, grasped hold of the knob, and hesitated. *You got this.* I pulled in a breath then pulled open the door. Chase stood there in jeans and a dark shirt, his hands buried in his pockets. I said nothing, just stepped back so he could enter.

He moved past me, the woodsy crisp scent of his cologne wafting by.

I fought to retain my composure and not let the recollections of our times together flood my brain.

"How're you doing, Valerie?" he asked.

She nodded. "I've been better."

He leaned against my desk and crossed his arms, like he had so many times before. Only, this time felt different. He felt like a stranger occupying my space.

I looked to Valerie. "Do you want me to leave you guys alone?"

She shook her head. "Please stay."

For a split second, Chase glanced to me before his eyes moved back to Valerie. "So, why'd you need me to come here?"

She looked to me as I sat down on the edge of Chantel's bed, nodding my support.

"I know what happened to Sydney Lane."

His mouth parted. "You do?"

She nodded. "But if I tell you, I need to know what's going to happen to me for not telling what I knew from the beginning."

"Well, it depends on your part in it."

"I didn't do it," she said.

"I'm not saying that. I'm saying if you were an accomplice in any way, there will be repercussions. If you just failed to divulge what you knew, you could be looking at a Class A misdemeanor."

She glanced to me, fear heavy in her eyes.

"Val, you want to do this. For you, for Sydney, for Sydney's family," I reminded her. "Officer Shaw will make sure that you're shown leniency for cooperating with the police." I glared at Chase. "Right, Officer Shaw?"

He winced at the tone of my voice and use of his real name. Then he nodded. "I'll do whatever I can," he assured her.

She said nothing, considering what he'd said and what she was about to do.

"The entire time I was here, I couldn't get a lead," Chase said, as if totally thrown off kilter that Valerie had the information he needed all along. "Sydney's parents were sure the Alpha Phis had something to do with her death. They needed someone who could get close."

"Oh my God. Chantel," I said, not meaning to say it out loud. But it finally made sense why he couldn't completely cut ties with her.

He nodded regrettably, before looking back to Valerie. "You'd be helping this case tremendously, Valerie."

She nodded, and her words came slowly as she stared at everything but Chase and me. "Sophia was right about the Alpha Phis taking their pledges up to the roof for initiation. But it's not done at Salvador Hall and it's not done as a group. It's done one at a time right up on this roof where most of the pledges live. They undress and stand on the ledge of the roof. Then, they recite the names of every chapter president who came before them." Tears dropped from Valerie's eyes and trailed down her cheeks. "Sydney was scared of heights. I remember her begging Chantel not to make her go up there, but Chantel wants things done her way. And she doesn't like it when people don't go along with her ways." Valerie wiped her nose with the sleeve of her shirt. "She forced Sydney up there, threatening to not make her a sister if she failed this final task."

A tear trailed down my cheek, the vision of the night feeling so real in my mind.

"Sydney's legs were shaking so badly as she stood up there. I went to try to help her. I was gonna hold her hand to steady her. But Chantel screamed at me to step back. She must've startled Sydney because…" Valerie swallowed, her tears falling freely now. "…she fell." She closed her eyes tightly. "I can still hear her screams in my nightmares."

I pushed away the tears that fell from my own eyes.

"Why didn't you call for help?" Chase asked.

"I tried. But Chantel grabbed my phone. She said we'd go to jail. She said we'd never see the light of day. I didn't believe her. I knew the truth would set us free. But she was worried about herself."

I shook my head, everything between Chantel and Valerie's exchanges making so much sense now.

"Chantel's father's a lawyer," Valerie explained. "So, she called him. He told her to get off the roof and play dumb. I was the only one standing in her way. I was the wildcard who could ruin her at any time because, unlike her, I had a conscience. And she knew it. She threatened to release the video of me hazing pledges, so I'd get kicked out of school—even though she's the one who made me do it. She used the secret against me, holding it over me whenever she could. I didn't know what to do. I had no one to talk to. I was so scared."

"Then she released the video anyway," Chase said.

Valerie nodded. "She wanted to keep me quiet. I think she was getting scared I'd crack."

Chase's breath whooshed through his lips. "This was not what I was expecting."

"Will I be arrested?" she asked, her eyes wild and scared.

"It's your word against hers. And you're right. Her father's a lawyer. One of the best in Texas. She could beat this charge if her story's plausible. You might not. You could be their scapegoat."

Valerie buried her face in her palms.

I rushed over and wrapped my arms around her, pulling her into my side. "You were so brave to tell the truth. You did the right thing. Chantel doesn't have this hanging over you anymore. You're free."

"I shouldn't have waited. I owed it to Sydney. And I owed it to her parents."

An image of Sydney's mom flashed in my mind's eye. She'd known her daughter. And she'd known her daughter would never harm herself. She'd been right. I couldn't wait for her to learn the truth.

"We can't tell anyone," Chase said.

Valerie and I both looked to him with our brows drawn. "Why not?"

"We need her confession," he said.

"She'll never confess," Valerie said.

"Don't be so sure," he said.

CHAPTER THIRTY-TWO

Valerie walked Chase to the door a short time later. "Thank you for not arresting me."

He nodded.

"Do you mind waiting a minute? I've just gotta grab something in my room." She hurried out the door before he could even respond.

The door closed behind her, leaving Chase and me alone and in complete silence. I think we both knew she wasn't coming back.

He moved toward my desk and leaned against it while I remained seated on my bed.

My pulse quickened, the muffled sound filling my ears. Could he hear it? Because it's all I could hear.

"So?" I said, needing to break the uncomfortable silence.

"So," he said.

"You're a cop." I just needed to say it so my brain could finally wrap itself around the knowledge.

"I am."

"Are you married?" I asked.

He buried his hands in his front pockets and shook his head.

"Do you have a girlfriend?"

He shook his head.

"Was I just part of the job?" I asked.

His eyes met mine. "It's complicated."

"I can keep up."

He closed his eyes for a long moment. "This was only my second big assignment. I'm young, right out of the academy, and they knew I could pass for a college student. Shoot. If I didn't go to the academy, I'd still be in college." He dragged his fingers through his hair the way he always did when he was conflicted. "I never expected to meet a girl who I'd actually have feelings for. This was supposed to be a job. A three-month job. But, when the trail ran dry on Sydney last year, they realized I might still be useful on campus since they had a growing drug problem the dean wanted to take care of. So, they sent me back this semester. I wasn't even supposed to be here. I wasn't even supposed to meet you."

"But you did."

He nodded.

"And you can't just pretend you didn't."

"I know," he said, seemingly pained by the notion.

"So, stop being an asshole and talk to me."

"What do you want to hear?"

"The truth."

He walked over and sat beside me. The dipping of the mattress pulled me closer to him, but I righted myself and kept my distance. "My feelings for you were real, Soph."

Tears pricked my eyes. I don't know what I expected him to say, but that wasn't it. "*Were* real?"

He grabbed my hands and held them. "*Are* real."

"You lied."

"I had to. You've gotta know that."

"You haven't called."

"I didn't think you wanted me to," he said, his eyes riveting between mine, looking for the slightest indication of how I truly felt. "Did you?"

I was so damned confused. So much had happened. So much deception. So much back and forth. "I need to know what was real and what wasn't."

"My last name and me ever wanting anything to do with Chantel. Those were lies."

I scoffed. "Thank God."

"The truth? There's a lot more of that. I am from Houston but I have my own apartment which is so much better than that awful frat house."

"Is that where you took off to when you disappeared?"

"Yeah. Those were mandatory training sessions and briefings I had to attend."

I nodded, understanding he had responsibilities.

"I did play football growing up. I even played my first two years in college before I changed paths and went to the police academy." He leveled me with his eyes. "I don't have a girlfriend or wife. I don't even have a dog. Chase is my real name. And I've got a lot of groveling to do to win back the reason I'm about to finally crack this case. The reason I loved getting up in the morning and attending classes I didn't even need. The reason I still smile just thinking about our time together."

My eyes lowered to our conjoined hands. "It's not gonna be easy."

"Nothing worth having ever is."

CHAPTER THIRTY-THREE

Valerie and I sat at a table in the dining hall. Her normally styled hair, though concealed by the hood of her dark hoodie, hadn't been washed in days, and dark circles plagued her eyes.

"Val, you need to eat," I said.

She shook her head, sitting across from me with crossed arms, staring off into space.

"This isn't healthy."

She said nothing.

"Hey, Val," Tina said as she passed by our table.

Valerie didn't acknowledge her roommate as she continued to stare off into space.

Tina glanced to me with worried eyes, knowing as I did, that Val had been skipping all her classes for days.

I shrugged, the only answer I could give her, then looked back to my friend. "Do you think you'd like to go to health services?"

Valerie's eyes flashed to mine.

"They have counselors you could talk to. It wouldn't hurt."

She cocked her head, her eyes pleading with me not to treat her like some fragile little flower.

I held up my hands in surrender. "It was just a thought." She'd been through a lot. Talking to someone could help her.

I walked her back to her room a little while later, making sure Tina was there. I knew better than to leave her alone. So did Tina at this point.

I returned to my room and finished my Art History essay in record time.

My phone buzzed. I checked the screen, not recognizing the number. "Hello?"

"Is this Sophia?" Chase asked.

My nose wrinkled at his question. "Yes."

"Hey, this is Chase Shaw," he said. "I got your number from this other guy Chase I used to know."

I stifled a grin, understanding what he was doing. "Oh yeah?" I lay back on my bed. "And what did this other Chase say that made you call me?"

"Well…he said you were a hell of a soccer *and* pool player."

"Go on."

"And you like football which is fucking hot."

I chuckled.

"He did mention that you have this list of things you hope to accomplish before you graduate college."

"I do."

"I was thinking…maybe you need someone to help you with some of those things."

I closed my eyes, feeling like a tween again when the boy I liked smiled at me. "I may."

"Anything in particular I may be an expert at?"

"I've still yet to dye my hair blonde."

"Not quite what I was thinking."

I laughed. "*Hmmm*. I'm gonna have to think about it," I said. "I mean, I don't really know you." I wasn't lying.

"I'm actually a really nice guy," he assured me, keeping up the charade.

"Says who?"

"Well…my mom, for one."

I laughed, thinking back to the cute picture of him and his parents in his room at the frat. "An *unbiased* source."

"Oh, my mom is as unbiased as they come. Maybe I could introduce the two of you sometime."

My heart flipped over in my chest. Did he really want us to meet? Was he trying to prove this thing between us—or at least what could be between us—was still important to him? But the bigger question was…could I forgive him and move past the deception? Could we really just pick up where Chase Reed and I left off? "We'll have to see how our first date goes."

"So, you're saying I can take you out?" he asked.

"You know where to find me."

His laughter carried through the phone, and one of the cracked pieces of my heart slipped back into place. I disconnected the call, cutting off his laughter before I did something foolish like invite him over.

My priority was Valerie. And she needed me.

CHAPTER THIRTY-FOUR

I was jerked awake by banging on my door Sunday night. I jolted up, my eyes shooting around my pitch-black room. Had I been dreaming?

The banging started up again.

I slipped out of bed and opened the door.

Tina stood there. "Valerie's gone."

"What do you mean gone?"

"She went to sleep when I did, but now her bed's empty," Tina said, on the verge of tears.

"Okay. Let me think. Did you check with the other girls?"

She nodded. "No one's seen her."

"Chantel?"

"I can't find her."

"Text her."

She nodded.

I grabbed my shoes and slipped them on. "I think I might know where Val went. You stay here and wait in case she comes back."

Tina nodded. "I knew something was wrong with her. I just didn't know how to help her."

"I know. I'm sure she knows too." I slipped out of my room and headed to the stairwell. Instead of going down, I climbed my way to the top floor and to the emergency exit.

Here goes nothing.

I pushed open the door which led to the roof. I'd never been out there before, but similarly to the roof Chase and I had been on, this one was flat with a ledge wrapping around the perimeter.

I squinted, struggling to see anything in the darkness. I pulled out my phone and turned on the flashlight, shining it around the dark space. Big vents, air ducts, and utility boxes filled different areas on the roof.

"Val?" I called out softly as I switched off my light. I didn't want to startle her, knowing how something like that ends. I moved around the vast area slowly, my legs trembling with each step. "Are you out here?" I called.

"Sophia?"

I spun around, searching for her voice. "I'm here. Where are you?"

"Up here."

Up? My legs almost gave out beneath me as I found her standing on the ledge. "Oh, dear God."

"Don't come any closer," she warned.

"Val? I need you to come down. Nothing good could come from you being up there."

"I can't take it anymore."

"What can't you take?" I asked.

"I feel like I'm cracking. I've got so much weighing me down."

"Like what, honey? What's weighing you down? I can help."

"Valerie?" Chantel's voice said from behind me.

I froze to my spot, my limbs turning numb.

"What are you doing?" she asked Valerie, anger coloring her tone.

"I can't take it anymore," Valerie said.

"Be smart, Valerie," Chantel warned.

"This is the first smart move I've made in a long time," Valerie assured her.

"Val, please come down. We can help you," I said.

"There's no helping me," she said. Even in the darkness the tears falling from her eyes were impossible to miss.

"You're scaring me. Please come down," I said.

"I need to do this. I need to be free," she said. "It's the only way."

"I don't understand," I said.

"Chantel knows."

My eyes shot to Chantel. "What do you know?"

She shrugged. "I have no idea."

"Well, you need to do something because apparently this has something to do with you," I said.

"You know what we did, Chantel. You know we were up here when Sydney fell," Valerie said.

"She's out of her mind," Chantel said.

"Don't you dare say that about her when she's up there," I spat. "Help her, God dammit!"

"Come down, Valerie," Chantel said. "We can get you help."

"Help?" Valerie scoffed. "You're the one who's gonna need help. You're the one who's going to have two dead bodies on your conscience—if you even have one."

"What happened to Sydney was an accident, and you know it," Chantel said.

"Then why did you force me to hide the truth? Why wouldn't you let me tell the police?" Valerie asked, the desperation in her voice heartbreaking.

"You know why we couldn't tell. We'd be pulled out of school or worse put in jail," Chantel said.

"Her parents needed to know the truth," Valerie said. "It was an accident. An accident I should've never allowed you to make me stay quiet about."

"How do you sleep at night?" I asked Chantel.

Her eyes cut to mine. "Don't go getting all self-righteous now, Sophia. Especially after you stole my boyfriend right out from under me."

"I was never your boyfriend," Chase said as he stepped out from behind one of the utility boxes.

"What the hell?" Chantel said, her head whipping around.

"Please come down from there, Valerie," Chase said, speaking for both of us.

Valerie hopped down and I breathed a huge sigh of relief. So many things could have gone wrong causing her to meet the same fate as Sydney. She slipped her phone from her pocket and recorded Chase as he moved toward Chantel.

"You have the right to remain silent," Chase began, pulling out his handcuffs. Chantel's eyes grew wild with fear as he approached. "Anything you say can and will be used against you in a court of law."

Chantel backed away from him. "You can't do this."

"I can and I will," he assured her as he grasped her by the shoulders and turned her around, cuffing her hands behind her back.

"Just in case," Valerie said as she continued to record the whole scene on her phone. "You never know when you'll need a video like this."

"My father will sue you for all you've got," Chantel spat at all of us.

"Why?" Chase asked. "You just gave me the confession I needed. And I assure you, I will take the stand to be sure you get the harshest punishment possible." He glanced to Valerie and me. "Thanks for the assist."

We nodded, watching as he walked Chantel toward the door to the roof, disappearing into the darkness.

Val stopped recording and turned to me, wrapping her arms around me tightly. "We did it."

"You did it," I assured her.

CHAPTER THIRTY-FIVE

It was late afternoon when I finally stepped outside my dorm. The previous night had been…a lot. News vans and cameramen had been camped outside since the early morning, occupying both the road and sidewalk.

"The case of Sydney Lane came to a close early this morning when the truth about a hazing accident surfaced," a reporter said into her camera. "In a sorority pledge event gone horribly wrong, Sydney fell unexpectedly to her death."

I dragged in a deep breath as I opened the passenger door to the black SUV waiting down the road for me.

"Hi," Chase said as I slipped into his passenger seat.

"Hi."

His eyes moved over my jeans and hoodie. "You look nice."

"Nice?"

He smirked. "It's a first date. I'm trying to be a gentleman." He reached over and linked our fingers.

Boy, I missed the feel of him. "Where are we going?"

"Just a little road trip, if that's okay?"

I nodded, curious where he planned to take me.

We drove for some time. My curiosity grew the longer we drove, but Chase kept me occupied by answering every question I asked him about himself.

"Spanish and Italian," he said, his eyes alternating between the road and me.

"So, you speak three languages?"

"And a little French."

"I'm impressed."

"That I'm smart?"

I laughed. "That you're so well-rounded."

"You know I could make a dirty joke right there, right?"

I rolled my eyes.

"How old were you when you first had sex?"

"Sixteen with Jessica Hynes."

I lifted a brow as jealousy whirled in my belly. "Do you see Jessica now?"

He pegged me with his eyes. "You jealous?"

"Maybe."

"I like that you're jealous."

"Where did it happen?"

"Where did we have sex?"

I nodded, cringing before he even answered since I knew it would only increase my jealousy.

"My friend's pool house. But, I assure you, it lasted two minutes and was definitely unmemorable for her."

I laughed to myself, his answer making me feel slightly better. "Favorite all-time song?" I asked, needing to change the subject before I did something crazy like go all stalker-mode on Jessica Hynes to see what she looked like or if she had a boyfriend.

"Good question. Maybe…'Sweet Home Alabama' or House of Pain's 'Jump Around'."

"Those are two extremes."

His low chuckle filled the SUV. "I've got eclectic tastes."

A comfortable silence passed between us as I considered what other information I wanted to know.

"Have you ever killed anyone?"

He hesitated. "Not yet."

The word *yet* reminded me what a dangerous job being a police officer really was. "Are you going to become a detective?"

"Someday," he said. "Right now, I'm good doing what I'm doing." His eyes cut to mine, and I got the feeling we weren't still talking about his future.

A short while later, he drove into a residential neighborhood filled with beautiful brick homes. He pulled into a long driveway and shifted into park.

I turned to look at him as he cut the engine.

His eyes held indecision.

"I don't have to meet your mom tonight," I assured him.

He shook his head. "That's not what this is."

My eyes widened. "Jessica Hynes?"

He shook his head with silent laughter. "Not even close." He turned, his attention seeking something by the front door.

I followed his gaze. I stilled, the hair on the back of my neck prickling.

Sydney's mother stood on the front steps, her arms wrapped tightly around her chest.

I pushed open my door before I even knew what I was doing. My legs carried me up the winding brick sidewalk toward her.

"Sophia," Mrs. Lane said, enfolding me in her arms. "My angel."

I blinked back stinging tears as her frail body held me to her. "I'm so happy you got the closure you were seeking."

She pulled back, still grasping my shoulders so she could look at me. Her eyes softened in the corners.

"Officer Shaw said you were the reason we learned the truth."

"I only helped Valerie. She's the one who fought to get you the truth. She's so sorry she couldn't get it for you sooner."

Mrs. Lane shook her head, holding back her own tears. "We're just happy we know now."

Chase stepped up beside me and Mrs. Lane wrapped her arms tightly around him. "Thank you, Officer Shaw. A weight has been lifted from our hearts."

He stepped out of her arms. "I was just doing my job."

"Yes, but we know being undercover and spending time with that dreadful girl had to take its toll."

He glanced to me. "Yeah, well, it led me to someone else."

She smiled, and Chase and I could see the genuine gratitude she felt for both of us in that moment. And if I didn't know any better, I'd say she was giving us her blessing.

* * *

I rested my head back against the headrest and closed my eyes.

"What are you thinking?" Chase asked as we drove back to Houston.

"I just can't shake the look on her face."

He nodded. "They've been waiting for the truth for a long time."

"How'd you know she'd want to see me?" I asked.

"I didn't. But I knew you'd want to see her."

Contentment filled my body. Sydney's mother finally got the truth. And, Chase knew me. And he knew exactly what I needed.

His eyes jumped between the road and me. "You once told me you wanted to be the reason someone did something amazing."

I nodded.

"I'd say you've done something amazing for that family. *And*, you got Valerie to step up and do the right thing to bring Chantel down. So, I'd say you accomplished your goal."

My head fell to the side and I stared at Chase, his side profile distinct in the fading evening light. "Take me to your apartment."

Surprise filled his eyes. "Yeah?"

I nodded.

We fell through his apartment door a little while later, our mouths incapable of disengaging as he kicked the door shut behind us. He walked me backward down his hallway to his bedroom, his lips moving desperately over mine. When the backs of my knees hit the bed, he lowered me down. Only then did he pull away. He stood at the foot of his bed and gazed down at me. My hair must've been a mess, my cheeks were beyond pink, and my chest heaved like a marathon runner.

I watched as he pulled his shirt over his head. I drank in the definition he had freaking everywhere. He slipped the button through the slot on his jeans and lowered his zipper. I watched every calculated move he made as he slowly pulled down his jeans and boxers and stepped out of them, standing naked in front of me.

A rush of desire swarmed in my chest. I may have thought I wanted him before. I may have thought I'd never feel more desire than I did when I asked him to sleep with me on my birthday. But I was wrong, and I understood that now. The feelings exuding from me as I lay on his bed with him offering himself to me for the first time couldn't be replicated. Nerves were a distant memory. This was what was supposed to happen. And, I'd never felt more sure until this moment.

I unzipped my hoodie and pulled it, along with the shirt beneath it, over my head.

Chase's eyes never wavered from mine. Even seconds later as I reached behind my back and unfastened my bra, letting it fall off my arms, his eyes remained on mine. I unbuttoned my jeans, lifted my ass, and shimmied out of them and my panties, leaving me just as naked as he was—except I still wore my mason jar necklace.

"You sure?" Chase asked.

I nodded, never more sure about anything. I lifted my hand and beckoned him closer with my index finger.

He crawled up the bed until he hovered over me. "I didn't think I could want you more than I did when you corrected my threat outside the frat house."

"Liar."

He shook his head. "And it only doubled when I walked into your room and found you watching football."

"Doubled, huh?"

"And, then it multiplied when you asked me to take you back here. I'm done."

"Done?"

He inched down so his lips were a mere breath from mine. "In love." He closed the distance, pressing his lips to mine. I wrapped my arms around him, arching into him and deepening the kiss. Our tongues were in sync, tangling as we explored each other's mouths. Our lips stayed molded together as our naked bodies found a rhythm.

I pulled out of the kiss, my heart racing and my chest heaving. "I'm ready,"

My breath hitched as his hand slipped between us, his fingers sliding between my folds.

"You *are* ready," he mused.

"I guess I missed you."

"What a nice surprise," he said.

"There's that word again," I said.

"Yeah, well, this is going to be a lot better than nice. I can assure you of that." He reached for his nightstand and slipped a condom out of the drawer, tearing it with his teeth, and reaching down to roll it on.

My pulse sped. This was happening. *We* were happening.

Chase braced his weight on his elbows beside my head and gazed down at me. "This means something to me, Soph."

"I know."

"Do you?"

I nodded.

"I needed to wait to do this until you knew the real me."

My heart constricted. I didn't know if I could take any more of his honesty.

"Tell me if I'm hurting you."

"I'll be fine," I said.

He captured my lips in a delicious kiss as his hips began to roll. He shifted slightly so his erection moved between my legs, slipping over my folds. He wasn't trying to push inside me yet. He was teasing me with the sensations he was creating each time he hit my clit. He didn't stop kissing me, even when I felt the tip press against my entrance. I sucked in a sharp breath, but he captured it with his lips, deepening the kiss as his hips thrust a little harder. My knees fell open, and that's all it took. He pushed once, then twice, then one more time before he stretched me wide. I groaned as Chase abandoned my lips and gazed down at me, gauging my expression. "You good?"

I nodded, not sure if it hurt or felt amazing to be connected to him in this way.

"Can I move?" he asked.

I nodded.

He started off slow, likely gauging my face and pinched eyes for pain as he moved in and out of me. Once I was used to the feel of him, I opened my eyes. He stared down at me with hooded eyes. I found myself too lost in those eyes to notice any pain. I slipped my hands behind his back, coasting them up and down his smooth skin. I lowered my hands to his ass, loving the feel of him clenching as he moved in and out of me. He shifted his hips again, and he hit a spot inside me that sent my legs trembling. "Do that again," I breathed.

He moved again, hitting the same spot.

My back arched off the bed and my head pressed into the pillow. "Oh, my God, yes."

His lips quirked, continuing his rhythm, in and out, faster and harder, hitting that spot and making me see stars. My eyes pinched tight. My body's internal spring began to coil. A rush of sensations twisted up inside of me. I held my breath. And as he thrust into me a few more times, the twisting released, and the sensations rippled out, sending tremors rushing to all parts of my body. I felt a warmth spread over me as my body quivered. This was so much better than what we'd done in my dorm room. Chase continued pounding into me, chasing the euphoria he'd given me. He groaned into my neck as his hips stopped moving and he stilled inside of me, his body going rigid. With his breathing labored, he lifted his head and pressed his forehead to mine. "Holy. Shit," he breathed.

I chuckled as he lowered himself on top of me. I held his sweaty body to me, enjoying the feel of our breaths working in tandem. This was what I'd waited for. Chase was everything I waited for. He was everything I needed. And everything I wanted.

"You think you want to do that again?" he asked.

"I think I want to do that all the time with you."

He laughed. "Does that mean I'm forgiven?"

"Depends."

He lifted his head and rested his chin on my chest. "On what?"

"Are you taking me skydiving?"

His eyes widened.

"Don't tell me you're scared."

He tipped his head. "Do I look scared?"

"You look hot. And, I'm kind of wondering when we're gonna get to use your handcuffs."

He dropped back his head and laughter tumbled out of him. And when he laughed like that, I knew this thing with us was meant to be. And no matter how difficult a road it had been getting to this place, there was nowhere else in the world I'd rather be.

EPILOGUE
Two Years Later

Chase

I stood in the doorway of our bedroom, watching Sophia fixing herself in the mirror. Her hair hung in loose curls past her shoulders, her black graduation cap fixed in place on her head. The normally unflattering gown did nothing to detract from how fucking beautiful she was. I couldn't help beaming with pride as I drank her in, knowing how lucky I was she'd chosen me—even after how difficult I'd made things in the beginning.

After Chantel's trial, we decided there was no better way to celebrate the verdict than to move in together. The judge showed no leniency, finding Chantel guilty of concealing an accidental death, as well as blackmailing and causing duress to Valerie. He sentenced her to two years in prison—the severest punishment for the crimes she could get. And, the icing on the whole fucking cake was Chantel's father was disbarred for aiding in the cover-up and not disclosing his knowledge of the accident. The piece of shit deserved to suffer right along with his over-privileged daughter.

"Hey," Sophia said, spotting me in the doorway in my suit.

I knew I'd sweat my ass off in a dark suit at the outdoor ceremony, but I also knew it fit the momentous occasion. "You almost ready?" I asked. "You look amazing by the way."

She laughed. "Thanks."

I walked over and wrapped my arms around her, careful not to wrinkle her gown or bump her cap that seemed to be fixed in place by too many hairpins. "I'm so proud of you."

"Stop trying to make me cry," she said.

I stepped back releasing her from my arms. "What's that?" I asked with my gaze on something behind her.

She turned, following my gaze to the tall dresser in the corner of our room.

The MVP trophy she received after her soccer championship win stood proudly on top of it. My girl kicked some serious ass on a soccer field. I guess I should've known she would. From our first meeting, when she was drunk as all get out, she still put my ass in its place. So many nights after, I replayed that exchange in my head wanting to hate her for making me feel anything toward her. And so many days after, I tried getting the same reaction out of her. Because if she hated *me*, I couldn't fall for her. Right?

"What?" she asked, pulling me from my thoughts.

"Your mason jar. It looks like something's in it."

She squinted at the jar that sat beside her trophy, noticing I was right. There *was* something inside it. "What is it? We did everything."

I walked over and picked up the jar, examining the contents. "There's one more paper."

"There can't be."

She was right. We had done every last thing in that jar, but I handed it to her anyway. "Hurry up. We still have time before you graduate."

She unfastened the top of the jar and reached inside.

My heartbeat began to gallop like a fucking racehorse.

Her fingers snatched the folded-up sheet of paper that looked like all the rest had in the bottom of the jar. She looked to me.

I nodded my encouragement.

She unfolded the paper and read it aloud. "Marry Chase Shaw." Her eyes flashed up—make that down—to me now kneeling in front of her.

She gasped like I knew she would.

Man, I loved that sound.

"That's *my* wish, Soph," I said. "I've helped make your wishes come true, now I'm hoping you help make one of *my* wishes come true."

Tears glazed her eyes as she gazed down at me, staring at me with so much love—love I never thought was possible.

I grasped hold of her left hand. "I promise to make you happy every day for the rest of your life." My thumb brushed over the back of her hand, so smooth and soft like the rest of her body. "And I promise to be the reason you have new and exciting experiences whenever you want to have them, no matter how crazy they may be."

She laughed, and the happy tears in her eyes threatened to fall. "I told you not to make me cry."

I smiled up at her. "What do you say, Soph? Will you make me the happiest guy alive and marry me?"

Not needing a second to consider it, she nodded. "Yes."

I pulled the one-carat platinum ring I knew she'd love from my pocket and slipped it onto her finger. Before she could even admire it, I swept her up into my arms—this time not worrying about wrinkling her gown—and kissed her. The tears rolling down her cheeks added salt to our kiss. And though I didn't think anything could top our first kiss in the library when I didn't give her a chance to resist me—because I physically couldn't hold out any longer, this one held so much more. It held promises and assurances for our future together.

Sophia pulled back and stared into my eyes. "I love you. You're the reason so many good things have happened in my life."

The warmth of knowing I was thoroughly and completely loved by this amazing woman swept over me, and regardless of the circumstances that brought us together, I knew with much certainty that Sophia was my happily ever after.

It hadn't taken long after meeting her that I came to my senses and realized my happiness depended on *her* happiness—depended on making *her* wishes come true. That's when I knew I was too far gone to ever recover unscathed. And as much as I wanted to believe I was the reason for all the good things that happened in her life, I knew she would've done them without me. She was a fighter. And she'd been right. She didn't back down from any challenge.

And whether we were getting tattoos, riding in hot air balloons, skydiving, surfing, or I was helping her dye her hair blond (for that one month junior year until I couldn't take looking at her as a blonde any longer), I was the lucky guy who got to be by her side as she carried out every last wish on her bucket list. And that made me so fucking happy.

There was only one thing left to do—besides marry her. I needed to get her started on a new list that included *me* and all our future adventures. Because there wasn't a doubt in my mind, it was going to be one hell of a ride.

The End

MORE FROM J. NATHAN

For You Standalone Sports Series:
Book #1 *For Finlay*
Book #2 *For Forester*
Book #3 *For Crosby*
Book #4 *For Emery*

Savage Beasts Standalone Rock Star Series:
Book #1 *Kozart*
Book #2 *Treyton*

Standalones:
Seren
Something About You
I Just Need You
You're the Reason
Until Alex
Before Hadley
Since Drew

ACKNOWLEDGEMENTS

Thank you so much for taking the time to read Sophia and Chase's story. I hope you enjoyed it as much as I enjoyed writing it!

To all the bloggers and readers who share my books. Thank you so much! I could never do this without all of you!

To my wonderful ARC team members who take the time to read and review my books. I appreciate you and your friendship!

To my reader's group, *J. Nathan's Book Boyfriend Lovers*. Thank you for always being excited to hear about my new books. Your enthusiasm is what motivates me to write!

To my wonderful beta readers: Dali, Renee, Mimi Jean, Maria, Jill, Kim, Kerrie, and Heather. Thank you for your invaluable feedback. I'm so lucky to have such great minds looking out for me!

To my editor Stephanie Elliot. Thank you for always being there to tell me what I need to hear and to delete all my overused words. LOL!

To Gemma at Gem's Precise Proofreads. Thank you for catching all my last-minute mistakes and for always loving what I write.

To my final proofreader Peggy M. Thank you for making sure the final version of my book is as flawless as it can be. You are amazing!

To my wonderful PA Renee. Thank you for being you! And for letting me nag you at all times of the day with silly questions. And even if I roll my eyes at you, I still think you're one in a million!

To Kate Farlow at Y'all. That Graphic for not only creating a beautiful cover, but for creating all my teaser graphics as well. I'm so happy I found you!

To Michelle Lancaster @lanefotograf for the gorgeous photo of Andy Murray. Your work is incredible, and Andy completely brought Chase to life!

And last, but never least, to my family. Thank you for always loving and supporting me, especially with this wonderful journey I get the opportunity to embark on. I'm so lucky to have the most wonderful family in the world!

ABOUT THE AUTHOR

J. Nathan resides on the east coast with her husband and ten-year-old son. She is an avid reader of all things romance. Happy endings are a must. Alpha males with chips on their shoulders are an added bonus. When she's not curled up with a good book, she can be found spending time with family and friends, at soccer and baseball games, and working on her next novel.

9 7 9 8 9 8 6 7 0 2 7 2 8